Kukum

MICHEL JEAN

Kukum

TRANSLATED BY
SUSAN OURIOU

ARACHNIDE

Original title: *Kukum*
Originally published in French (Canada)
© Michel Jean (Agence littéraire Patrick Leimgruber), 2019
© Éditions Libre Expression, Montréal, Canada, 2019
All rights reserved
English translation copyright © 2023 Susan Ouriou

First published in English in 2023 by House of Anansi Press Inc.
houseofanansi.com

House of Anansi Press is committed to protecting our natural environment.
This book is made of material from well-managed FSC®-certified forests,
recycled materials, and other controlled sources.

House of Anansi Press is a Global Certified Accessible™ (GCA by Benetech)
publisher. The ebook version of this book meets stringent accessibility standards
and is available to readers with print disabilities.

27 26 25 24 23   1 2 3 4 5

Library and Archives Canada Cataloguing in Publication

Title: Kukum / Michel Jean ; translated by Susan Ouriou.
Other titles: Kukum. English
Names: Jean, Michel, 1960- author. | Ouriou, Susan, translator.
Description: Translation of: Kukum.
Identifiers: Canadiana (print) 20220497311 | Canadiana (ebook) 20220497397 |
ISBN 9781487010904 (softcover) | ISBN 9781487010911 (EPUB)
Classification: LCC PS8619.E2423 K8513 2023 | DDC C843/.6—dc23

Cover design: Marike Paradis
Typesetting: Lucia Kim
Photo credits: Carine Valin (36–37, 140); Bibliothèque et Archives nationales du
Québec (156: Herménégilde Lavoie; 173: J. H. Ross); Jeannette Siméon (171, 198);
Michel Jean (135, 207)

*House of Anansi Press is grateful for the privilege to work on and create from the Traditional
Territory of many Nations, including the Anishinabeg, the Wendat, and the Haudenosaunee,
as well as the Treaty Lands of the Mississaugas of the Credit.*

 Canada Council   Conseil des Arts
for the Arts   du Canada

 ONTARIO ARTS COUNCIL
CONSEIL DES ARTS DE L'ONTARIO
an Ontario government agency
un organisme du gouvernement de l'Ontario

With the participation of the Government of Canada | Canadä
Avec la participation du gouvernement du Canada

*We acknowledge the financial support of the Government of Canada through the National
Translation Program for Book Publishing, an initiative of the Action Plan for Official
Languages—2018–2023: Investing in Our Future, for our translation activities.*

Printed and bound in Canada

MIX
Paper from
responsible sources
FSC
www.fsc.org   FSC® C103567

In memory of France Robertson

Apu nanitam ntshissentitaman anite uetuteian
muku peuamuiani nuitamakun
e innuian kie eka nita tshe nakatikuian.

"I don't always remember where I come from
in my sleep, my dreams remind me of who I am
my origins will never leave me."

JOSÉPHINE BACON
Tshissinuatshitakana
Bâtons à message (Talking Sticks)

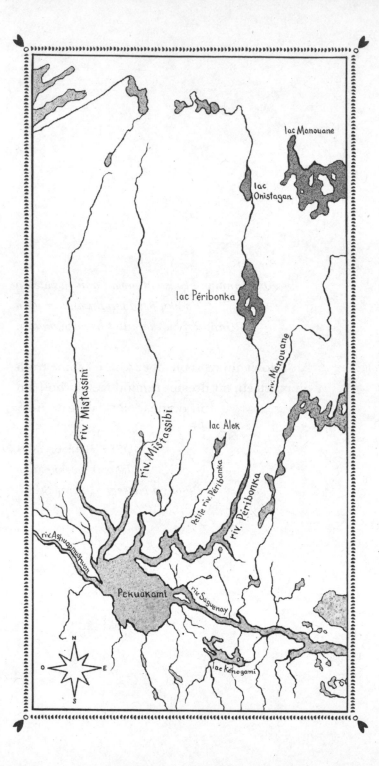

NISHK

A sea surrounded by trees. Water that goes on as far as the eye can see, grey or blue according to the sky's moods, crossed by icy currents. The lake is both beautiful and frightening. Grandiose. And life there is as fragile as it is intense.

The sun rises through the morning mist, but the sand is still permeated with the cool of night. How long have I sat here looking at Pekuakami?

A thousand dark dots dance between the waves and gossip insolently. The forest is a world of concealment and silences. Prey and predators vie with each other's skill at blending into their surroundings. However, the wind ferries the din of the migrating birds well before they appear in the sky, and nothing seems able to contain their honking.

Wild geese make an appearance around the time my memories with Thomas begin. We had left three days earlier, paddling northeast without straying from the safety of the shores. To the right, water. To the left, a line of sand and rocks looming ahead of the forest. I found myself between two worlds, in the thrall of a never-before-experienced intoxication.

When the sun started to set, we manoeuvred to shore in a bay sheltered from the wind. Thomas set up camp. I helped as best I could, peppering him with questions, but all he did was smile. Over time, I understood that, in order to learn, you have to watch and listen. There is no point in asking.

That evening, crouched back on his heels, on his lap the bird he had just shot, a plump specimen, he began to pluck it, starting with the biggest feathers. It's a task that requires meticulous attention since, if you go too fast, the shaft will break off and stay implanted in the flesh. It takes time. That's often the way in the woods.

Once he'd rid the creature of its plumage, he ran it through the fire to burn off all the down. Then, with the blade of his knife, he scraped the skin, without damaging it or its precious fat. Then he hung the goose over the flames to roast.

I made tea and we ate, seated on the sand facing the dark lake under a star-studded sky. I had no idea what awaited us. But, at that moment, I was sure that all would go well and that I had been right to follow my instincts.

He spoke almost no French and I no Innu-aimun. But that night, on the beach, enveloped in the aroma of grilled meat, at the seasoned age of fifteen, for the first time in my life I felt I had found my place.

I don't know how our people's story will end. But for me, it begins with that meal between the forest and the lake.

Taking Flight. Silkscreen print. Thomas Siméon

ORPHAN

I grew up in a world of sameness where the four seasons decided the order of things. A slow-paced universe where salvation came from a plot of land that had to be tilled over and over again.

My oldest memories are of the wood cabin we lived in, not much more than a simple settler's home, square with a two-sided roof and a single window on the front. Out that way, a sandy path. Out the back, a field clawed from the forest through sheer human exertion.

It's a rocky soil, yet men treat like a treasure; they work it, fertilize it, rid it of stones. In return, it provides nothing but tasteless vegetables, plus some wheat and hay to feed the cows, the givers of milk. The harvest would be either good or not. Everything came down to the weather. Heaven would decide, the priest would say. As though God had nothing better to do.

I have no memory of my parents. I would often try to picture their faces... My father, tall, burly, and resolute. With powerful hands. My mother, blond with blue eyes like my own. Delicate features, warm and loving. Of course, the two of them existed only in my child's mind. Who knows what the two who brought me into being were really like? It doesn't matter, in fact. But I like to think that they were endowed with strength and gentleness.

I grew up with a woman and a man I called "ma tante" and "mon oncle." I don't know whether they loved me, but they looked after me. They died a long time ago, and the house at the end of Rivière à la Chasse burned down. The land, however, is still there. There are fields everywhere. Now, farmers, holding tight to their tracts of land, surround Pekuakami.

The wind picks up and comes to lick my worn face. The lake heaves. I am no more than an old woman who has seen too much. At least they can do nothing to you, lake of mine. You are unchanging.

PEKUAKAMI

The sound of its whistle carries in the warm air, strident, uninterrupted.

The train shrieks from the minute it enters our community until it leaves, no matter the time of day or night. Now that they can no longer travel to their hunting grounds, many people have turned to the bottle. It happened that one or another would fall asleep on the railroad tracks. There were accidents. That is why the conductors slow down and blow the whistle so the Innu will clear the rails and let the train continue on its way.

I prefer to ignore it. I focus on the lake before me, its waves that bite into the sand and come to rest with a murmur at my feet. This morning, the wind carries the lake's mist, which dampens my skin. And so we are one, Pekuakami, the sky and me.

For close to a century, I have lived by its side. I know every bay and every river that flows to or from it. Its song covers the din of metal horses, soothes humiliation. Should it anger at times, its rage eventually wanes.

We respected it, feared its might, and no one

ventured out far offshore because the wind that comes up without warning can swallow careless canoes. Today, it has become more like a sports field on which humans play with their large motorboats. They have dirtied its water, they have emptied it of its fish. They even swim across it, have given it the name of a saint. They fail to respect its greatness.

However, Pekuakami is the only lake in Nitassinan that is impossible to see across. Just as with the ocean, you have to imagine the opposite shore. I can still picture that shore in my mind. When I close my eyes, the one the elders called Pelipaukau appears, the river of shifting sand. At the river's mouth, its water seems to stand still between pale sandbanks, so slowly does it move, as though its long journey down from the Otish mountains has wearied it.

Scenes from my first encounter with the river arise, and just as almost a hundred years ago, I feel a thrill. Still. I see myself in the canoe with him. We glide silently over its smooth surface. I am about to be plunged into a world of which I know only what he has told me. The first dizzying headiness is the most intoxicating.

He was not much older than me. But his gaze already held a wisdom and strength that won me over. Thomas told me about Rivière Péribonka with an economy of words I would come to appreciate. Although his lilting voice could seem hesitant at times, I never saw a man more sure of himself. As the canoe started up the river and the Péribonka unfurled ahead, my heart leapt.

Today, they have built a town, but in those days vast sandbars crowded the horizon. Like the Ashuapmushuan and Mistassini rivers, Rivière Péribonka opened a route to the north. It led us to the Siméons' hunting grounds.

The gentle flow of its estuary was misleading. Soon waves would swell, the current would accelerate, and ahead of us would appear impassable falls that had to be bypassed on foot. The river had several faces.

At journey's end lay the tapered lake Thomas had described, beyond the mountains whose summits loomed on the horizon. At the age of fifteen, it was still easy to dream. But what I was about to discover was more majestic than anything I could ever have imagined.

THE INDIAN

My uncle was one of those men who woke up before dawn day after day, downed a few biscuits and his scalding tea, and headed out to work in their fields. Short and stocky, he had a weathered face that always wore a worried expression. His huge hands, dotted with spots from hours spent in the sun, showed the signs of a life of hard labour.

My aunt wound her already grey hair into a bun on top of her head, which she felt gave her a distinguished look. Frail, her emaciated features betraying her fatigue, she was pious and accepting of the sacrifices to be made since "God gave us this land to take care of," she said.

Farm life is akin to a calling. Farmers believe their land protects them from the wilderness. In reality, it turns them into slaves. Children work the land like adults. I milked the cows every morning before school and on my return at day's end. I liked looking after the cows. I talked to them as I pulled on their teats. We understood one another, the cows and I. In the summer, I took them out to the field. It bordered a small river, and to the north, beyond the hills, was the lake.

On Sundays, we went to church in Saint-Prime. At that time, it was nothing but a plain building made of wooden planks with windows on either side and a silver bell where we froze in winter and suffocated in summer. We had no elegant outfits to wear like some did, but our clothes were clean. Out of respect for the house of God.

I earned good marks in school, and my aunt would have liked to see me become a teacher. But she and my uncle didn't have the means to send me to teacher training school. In any case, I couldn't imagine being cooped up inside, standing in front of a row of young people placed under my responsibility. At the same time, I couldn't see myself marrying the son of a Saint-Prime farmer either and raising a big family on a rocky plot of land. I preferred not to think about the future.

Slowly the village grew. New settlers arrived, drawn by the offer of free land that nevertheless had to be cleared. The parishioners talked of replacing the small church with a more imposing stone building topped by a vertiginous steeple that could be seen from afar. The mayor spoke of progress.

Everyone had that word on their lips. In reality, not much happened. More villagers only meant more men hitched to their ploughs and more women at their stovetops.

Sometimes in the evening, once I'd finished my chores, I'd watch the sun set behind the forest. What lay beyond the trees? Who lived on the other side of the great lake? Was that world any different from my own? Or was it just a succession of villages as dreary as ours was? When I returned home, my aunt would scold me.

"Why so late, Almanda? It's dangerous out at night. You could come across savages."

"Ma tante, really. There's no one around. Nothing to steal. Nothing to fear."

It was on one of those evenings as I milked the cows in the muted light of the setting sun that I saw him for the first time. It was early summer and a warm breeze swept through the tall grasses. A canoe appeared, silently gliding down Rivière à la Chasse. A bare-chested man with coppery skin paddled at a leisurely pace, letting the current carry him along. He didn't look much older than me, and from my vantage point I could see five wild geese laid out in his birchbark canoe. Our eyes met. He didn't smile. I wasn't afraid. The hunter disappeared round a bend, behind a hill.

Who was that young man? The geese must have drawn him this far in their flight since we had never seen any Indians here before. I finished the milking and took the path home through the fields. The wind dispersed the blackflies, which were many at that time of year. I was careful not to spill any milk. We needed it badly now that rain had pushed back the sowing season. My uncle and aunt were worried. Our life hung from such a thin thread.

The next day, the canoe reappeared at around the same time, once again full of geese fanned out on the bottom. The boy with almond eyes stared at me. I waved, and he acknowledged me with a nod. Sitting upright in his frail boat, he paddled easily, compelling in his silence. With my palms glued to a cow's teat, I watched him drift away.

When I rose at dawn the next day, the image of the mysterious hunter and his noble glide over the water still preoccupied me. Did he follow prey every day? Did he change grounds or, like farmers, did he always cultivate the same area? The questions troubled me all day long as I helped my aunt make bread, prepare the meals, mend clothing.

After supper, armed with my pail, I headed for the pasture, secretly hoping to catch a glimpse of the young man who seemed so unlike anyone I had ever known, and who I imagined as a kind of wanderer letting the wind show him the way. I was young, of course. With no one around me but people who were prisoners of their land, I had suddenly come across someone who was free. So it was possible.

That summer evening, as I stepped into the pasture, he sat waiting for me on the fence with the patience of someone who cares nothing for time's passing. The wind ruffled his hair, calling attention to his shy expression—that of a child. We were both children. He watched as I drew near. I spoke first.

"Hello."

He answered with a nod, his gaze intent. Did he even know how to smile?

"What's your name?"

He hesitated for a second. "Thomas Siméon."

He had a gentle, lilting voice.

"I'm Almanda Fortier."

Once again, he nodded. The solidity and strength emanating from him contrasted with his reserved manner. As though two people lived inside him at once.

"Did you come by canoe?"

"Not today."

He groped for words. "The wind…"

"Did you walk from Pointe-Bleue?"

Another nod.

"Hey, that's quite a long way!"

"Not really."

It was over ten kilometres to Pointe-Bleue. I couldn't imagine walking all that distance. But when the wind blows as it did that day, no one dares venture out on the water. He had had to walk in order to see me. That impressed me.

We talked and, with a great deal of effort, managed to make ourselves understood. His natural kindness pleased me from the start. Thomas told me that he'd canoed up Rivière à la Chasse the other day to follow the geese.

"Do you like goose?"

I'd never had it before. "My uncle doesn't hunt. He farms the land. Is it good?"

He seemed confused for a moment.

"Does it taste like chicken?"

He shrugged, then added, "Never had chicken."

We burst into laughter.

"Do you live in Pointe-Bleue?"

"Yes and no."

He tilted his head, trying to figure out how to express himself in my language.

"Pointe-Bleue is where we spend the summer. And sell furs to the Hudson Bay store. Where I live is over there."

He pointed to the northeast.

"You live on the lake?" I laughed, and he bristled. I was afraid I'd vexed him. "That was a bad joke. Sorry."

Beneath his shyness, there was an intensity that troubled me.

"Where we live," he continued, "is on the other side of Pekuakami."

Pekuakami. I had never heard Lac Saint-Jean referred to that way. I liked the name immediately.

"On the other side is Rivière Péribonka and, above it, a lake with the same name. And impassable waterfalls, Passes-Dangereuses. That's my home."

With his halting words, Thomas conjured up a world foreign to me. And the thought of that impetuous river rushing through the heart of the forest fascinated me.

That night over dinner, I asked my uncle what lay on the other side of Lac Saint-Jean.

"Nothing. There's nothing there. Just woods and flies."

"Do you know Rivière Péribonka?"

"Never seen it, but from what I've heard, it's a big one. There aren't any settlers up there. It's deep in the back country."

"And Passes-Dangereuses? Do you know that name?"

My uncle thought for a second, stroking his grey beard. "No. Never heard of 'em."

I went to bed that night with my head full of images of the forest straddling mountains on into infinity, and it was as though, in the distance, I could hear the roar of those menacing falls.

*

The next day, Thomas paddled over and pulled his canoe onto shore. Carrying a goose in his right hand, he climbed the hill slowly, confidently. With him, nothing was ever hurried.

"Here, *nishk*. You'll tell me if you like it."

My heart swelled. I had never before been given a present.

"Thank you, Thomas. That's so nice of you. You didn't have to."

He smiled. "*Nishk* is late this year. The winter was long."

I scanned his features, his oval face with its high cheekbones, his eyelids so narrow they gave him an intense gaze. His full lower lip lent his mouth a certain sensuality. He was taller than me, with broad, sturdy shoulders, very thick black hair, smooth dark skin.

"You? Have you hunted?"

"No. I don't know if I could kill an animal."

"You like meat?"

15

"Of course. I know. It makes no sense."

"I never kill for pleasure. Always to eat."

He lifted up the bird and smoothed its ruffled feathers.

"*Nishk* gave his life. You must only take what you need."

The wisdom expressed in those simple words revealed Thomas's goodness and generosity.

When I arrived home carrying the large goose, my aunt stared wide-eyed. "What's that, Manda?"

"A chicken."

"Where did you catch it, my girl?"

"I caught it in my hands as it flew. Like this."

I pretended to jump, my arms raised to the heavens. My aunt shot me a stern glance.

"Someone gave it to me."

She planted her fists on her hips.

"An Indian gave it to me. He's canoed by the pasture a couple of times on his way home from hunting."

"An Indian gave you a goose?"

Her voice went up.

"Well, yes, ma tante, he's nice. He had lots. It'll be a change from biscuits for us."

She took the bird, carried it into the kitchen and immediately started plucking it.

"You're right, Manda. Your uncle will be happy. Goose is good."

We often didn't have meat, especially in the summer, when it had to be salted and stored in barrels to keep. Thomas's gift came at a good time. It sent a celebratory fragrance through our smoky cabin. Neither my aunt nor my uncle asked anything more about him.

Over the following days, Thomas dropped by the pasture every evening. Mostly by canoe, sometimes on foot if the conditions forced him to. He spoke of his territory, and I told him about life in the village and about school, which he had never been to. He tried to teach me a few words of his language, but I wasn't a good student, which made him laugh.

His French didn't get much better than my Innu-aimun, but he was patient as he described his world to me. The trips as a family to their hunting grounds on Rivière Péribonka, the winter camp set up in the heart of the forest, their life trapping and travelling to the flat open country of the North to hunt caribou. And all the work required to preserve and store the animals' meat and hides. There were also evenings round the campfire, during which the elders told stories to amuse and educate the children. Finally, with spring melt, their return to the lake to reunite with those who, like them, had spent long months in the woods.

In Saint-Prime, most people thought of Indians as inferior beings. Yet Thomas's tales described a life that showed a different relationship to the earth, an existence graced with wide-open horizons, and the more he spoke, the more I longed for its fresh air.

"I'd like to see Rivière Péribonka and its mountains, Thomas."

"You wouldn't be afraid?"

"Yes, a little…But still…"

"I'd like you to come, Almanda. By canoe," he said, pointing ahead of him, "to my home."

I looked into the eyes of the person asking me to follow him to the ends of the earth. There I saw the river, the long lake, and in between, me and this broad-shouldered young man with his confident air.

POINTE-BLEUE

"Have you gone mad, Almanda?"

My aunt was a humble, hard-working woman. I had never before heard her raise her voice as she'd just done. "You're not going to marry an Indian. Do you know what it's like for them? They have a hard go of it in the woods. You're not used to that kind of life. It makes no sense, my girl."

I guess it did take a certain madness to leave for the woods with an almost-stranger, worse, a savage.

"I'll get used to it, and they'll teach me their language. Anyway, ma tante, look at us. It's not like we're living in luxury here. We've had no meat for two weeks now, nothing but buckwheat pancake to eat. You know I won't have a dowry toward a wedding, so what future is there for me here?"

My aunt was no doubt afraid for me. But nothing could change my mind, and it didn't take her long to realize it.

The next week, my uncle harnessed the horse to the buggy, and we left for Pointe-Bleue. He wanted to stop in Roberval first, though, to buy a scythe. The road was in good condition and the animal trotted at a fair clip down the hills. The sun rose over the lake, a warm breeze caressed my cheeks, and my heart raced as we put more distance between us and the farm.

Roberval was just a small country town, but the church, with its tall tinplate spire sparkling in the sky, was imposing. Posh-looking houses with fine painted porches lined the main street, bordered by wooden sidewalks. Women in long dresses cut from costly fabric protected their pale skin from the sun with pastel-coloured parasols. The men, dressed in dark suits, wore elegant felt hats.

"You should try one, mon oncle."

My aunt burst out laughing. My uncle jammed his straw hat down on his head, muttering something neither she nor I could make out.

The farm supply store was a good-sized building in which an industrious hustle and bustle reigned. In the yard, scythes and tillers of every size were carefully stored. My uncle stepped down and immediately headed for the main building. He came out a few minutes later with a man wearing a bowler hat, which I thought strange for someone who had farmers for customers. The merchant helped him find what he needed and carefully set the new tool in the back of the cart.

We headed north along a dirt road bordering the lake. Houses grew fewer and farther between. We advanced in the silence of the countryside. After a few kilometres, the road led to a strip of land sloping down to the shore. The wind had died, and the blue of the water merged with the blue of the sky. Ahead appeared a village like none I had ever imagined before.

Even though Saint-Prime was nothing more than a hamlet in the middle of nowhere, its buildings were disposed in an orderly fashion on either side of the main street. There was a general store and a few houses clustered round the church. In the distance could be seen the farms with their side buildings and their fences marking off the fields.

The village before me also had a church at its centre, a former chapel from the Métabetchouan mission that the oblate fathers had moved there ten years earlier, transporting it over the frozen surface of the lake. A store. A small square house with a sloping roof surrounded by a white fence that lodged the Hudson Bay Company's trading post. But there were no streets, no intersections. No elegant passersby hurrying along wooden sidewalks. There were only tents planted in the sand in no apparent order in front of the lake.

Thomas waited for us where Pointe-Bleue began, sitting on an embankment of tall grasses. He jumped to his feet and waved. My uncle raised his straw hat, my aunt nodded, and I smiled. Then I noticed the spark in his eye. The same one that would be there till the day he drew his last breath.

"Come," he said, his voice so soft it was like a whisper.

We left the horse and cart behind. People's expressions grew blank as we passed, and I could feel my aunt stiffen. Later, I would understand that what we had interpreted as unfriendliness was nothing but an expression of timidity on the part of the Innu in the presence of people from elsewhere. After a while, we reached a small camp several tents strong set up at the foot of a hill.

"My family," said Thomas.

The Siméon clan consisted of his father, Malek, his brother, Daniel, and his sisters, Christine and Marie. Each had their own tent. Thomas was the eldest and it showed.

Other than Thomas and Christine, no one spoke French. Our conversation amounted to no more than a few words. Malek was a short man with a weathered face and gnarled hands, his gaze still sporting the same spark that Thomas had inherited. Marie and Christine wore wide flowered skirts and checkered smocks. Both had a scarf tied round their neck on which a heavy metal cross hung. Their hair was knotted into imposing buns on either side of their head, and they wore beaded felt caps in bright red and black.

Thomas showed me his tent. Inside, a thick carpet of fresh fir boughs covered the ground.

"It's not very big," I blurted out.

Christine shot me a glance in which I read both curiosity and distrust. With hindsight, I realize how strange my attitude must have seemed to both my family and Thomas's. But, intoxicated by the images that Thomas had painted for me of a forest that went on for as far as the eye could see, I felt confident, convinced there was no future for me in Saint-Prime or, in any event, that if I stayed there nothing would change for me. That thought was unbearable. As it turned out, our modest house of wooden planks disappeared a long time ago. My uncle and aunt rest in peace in the small village cemetery, but cows still graze in their former fields, and morning and night, someone else looks after them.

What would my life have been like had a young almond-eyed hunter not ventured past there, drawn by a flock of wild geese in flight?

COMMITMENT

Péribonka is not a river. Not like Rivière à la Chasse, winding between banks of tall grasses. Péribonka is a route dug by giants through the rock. Its untamed and breathtaking nature freed me from the horizon.

I liked listening to the echo of my voice as it lost itself among the mountains. Thomas watched with a smile, never missing a stroke of the paddle.

He had described for me the world I was now discovering, all my senses heightened. The tangy scent of spruce, the deep blue of the river, the incandescence of the sun, the coolness of the air coming from the summits, the murmur of the canoe in the water.

After that trip to Pointe-Bleue, my uncle and aunt no longer objected to our union, even though I was barely fifteen. After all, Thomas was only eighteen. We were married in a simple ceremony held in the small chapel in Pointe-Bleue. I wore a white dress and he a grey suit that gave him a lawyerly look. The day was a happy one.

When the time came to give ourselves to each other, I felt his heart expand inside his chest, and knowing it beat so hard for me excited me. He laid me back on the fir needles with which he had carpeted the tent, and that woody fragrance will always be associated in my mind with him. His lips on my skin, his fingers exploring my naked flesh, his embrace, the movement of our impassioned and awkward bodies to the sound of nearby waves breaking and ebbing rocked the night.

I rolled Thomas over and squeezed his hips between my thighs. His gaze betrayed a trace of anxiety. His life too had been overturned. Ours was a shared headiness since I had never imagined a man offering himself as openly as I was prepared to do. But at that moment, with his whole being trembling beneath me, nothing seemed clearer.

Thomas promised I would never be alone. He kept his word, even though I sometimes hold it against him that he offered me a gift that would later be taken away. He couldn't have known that one day men would rob us of the forest and its rivers. All that remains of that treasure he ferried me to with the strength of his arms is Pekuakami. Every morning, I walk to the shore of blond sand to gather my thoughts. A way to keep a bit of Thomas alive inside.

But late that summer, we were preparing to overwinter on what was still the Siméons' hunting grounds. For our first trip there together, he had decided we would leave a week after the others and catch up with them at Passes-Dangereuses. That would be our honeymoon.

The trip took a month. After hugging the northernmost shoreline of Pekuakami, we headed up the river. To cross several rapids, we pushed the canoe along using long wooden poles. Often, however, we had to give up, stop, remove all the gear and carry everything on our backs through the woods.

We'd put the canoe in the water early each morning, then paddle in tandem till late afternoon, when we'd set up camp for the night. Thomas already knew the places to pitch our tent. He knew the route by heart, and I was fascinated that, despite his youth, he had so much knowledge. It took years for me to learn how to walk through the forest without getting lost.

PÉRIBONKA

On that first trip, we brought only the strict min-imum. Even that made for a good deal of gear. The bags' straps hurt, but even though I wasn't as sure-footed as Thomas on the rocks we had to climb, I never complained.

One of the most trying ordeals required a day-long hike. We had to climb a mountain through the forest following a trail blazed by generations of hunters. I matched Thomas's slow pace. Perspiration stung my eyes, and my mouth filled with salt, but I refused to ask him to relieve me of part of my load.

The steep descent was even more perilous. We had to skirt high cornices carrying our heavy load. I had vertigo, which amused Thomas, who, as someone who had grown up on these trails, could not begin to understand my irrational reaction.

The portage took two days through the mountains and the forest. Finally, on the third morning, we were able to put the canoe back in the water and, in short order, leave behind the rapids hemmed in by stone cliffs, their rumbling soon lost to nature.

After thirty minutes, the forest had regained that strange calm in which time stands still. My muscles ached, and I had trouble keeping a grip on the paddle with my blistered palms. We paddled all day long listening to the silence of Nitassinan.

That evening, as we set up camp on a point of sand for the night, Thomas decreed we would stay put for three days. "I have to teach you how to hunt, Almanda. Like a real Innu woman."

That was the first time he spoke of me as being Innu. Maybe that was when I became one.

THE WINCHESTER

My uncle owned a shotgun, but neither my aunt nor I were allowed to touch it. Firearms were reserved for men in Saint-Prime. Not here. Thomas showed me how to load a rifle, how to lodge the butt in the hollow of my shoulder and take aim keeping both eyes open.

I practised shooting onshore. After an hour, I began to feel more comfortable with the weapon.

"You've got a good eye, Almanda."

I reloaded the Winchester, took aim at the stone he'd set on a rock and pulled the trigger. The stone flew apart, and I shrieked with joy. Thomas had a hint of pride in his eye.

"You're ready for partridge. There are quite a few around here."

We set out along the river. We did our best to blend in with our natural surroundings, and I tried to copy his slow progress but felt clumsy. Thomas followed a stream whose banks, covered in a spongy moss, absorbed the sound of our footsteps.

We'd advanced without speaking for a good hour

when a creature erupted from a bush, frantically beating its wings. The shot rang out, and the bird, now as heavy as stone, hurtled to the damp ground. The entire scene couldn't have lasted more than a few seconds. Instinctively, Thomas had followed its trajectory with his rifle. By evaluating the speed of its flight, he was able to hit his target. A second's hesitation on his part and the partridge would have escaped. Killing a creature mid-flight seemed so much harder than shooting an unmoving object. Would I manage it?

We returned to camp, and I plucked and prepared the partridge, something I'd learned to do with the hens at the farm. Thomas cooked it fanned out over a few branches above the fire.

We had only covered a third of the distance to Passes-Dangeureuses. We still had long weeks of travel ahead and already I was exhausted. The river, quite wide at that spot, flowed slowly. On the opposite bank, a mother moose and her baby emerged from the woods and approached the water to drink. The little one, nervous and clumsy, made a sprint for the river and stopped short. It hesitated a second, looking left then right, then jumped in and plunged its head underwater, then up again, projecting white spray over its back. Her senses on alert, the calf's mother surveyed their surroundings. It was risky for them to come out from cover.

The wind blew in our direction, and she hadn't spotted us.

"Mush."

"*Mush?*"

"*Mush*," he said, pointing at the two moose.

I repeated the word and the roundness of its sound while the baby played under its mother's attentive gaze.

"*Mush*," Thomas continued, "tastes good."

"I don't know if I could shoot a moose, Thomas. Especially not a baby's mother."

Taking a deep breath, Thomas rolled his eyes, then his gaze returned to the moose.

"By giving its life, *mush* allows the hunter to live. You have to thank it. Respect its sacrifice."

I had come from a world in which it was thought that man, created in the image of God, reigned from the top of the pyramid of life. Nature, offered up as a gift, was meant to be tamed. Here I found myself confronted with a new order in which all living beings were equal with man superior to none.

The mother moose snorted, and the little one leapt from the water. Playtime was over. With cautious steps, the two returned to the safety of the woods. Once again, we found ourselves looking out over Rivière Péribonka. The air, fragrant with the scent of pine, filled our lungs, and around us thousands of hearts of different shapes and sizes beat at the same time.

PILEU

The next day, we went out hunting again. This time to the south at the foot of the mountain. Thomas shot a partridge. I tried my luck a bit later. A large bird swooped down to scare us away from its nest. I took aim but hesitated just before shooting, and the bullet missed its target.

That evening, we made supper and ate on the shore watching the sun set behind the already white peaks. In the tent, stretched out on our bed, I relived the partridge swooping down on me. Instead of shooting, I had tried to take aim. By that time, it was too late. Lulled by Thomas's steady breathing, I played the scene over and over again in my mind. When I finally did fall asleep, the partridge still eluded me.

The next morning, our third in this camp, we tried our luck along the small river. Two days of rest had helped me recover, and I felt better. We advanced, surrounded by the cries of animals we never so much as glimpsed, as though they fled as we approached. For nearly three hours, we didn't see a living soul. Thomas didn't say a word, and I too kept quiet, listening to the frustrating din of nature.

On reaching a small waterfall, we crossed the river, stepping on moss-covered rocks. I made as little noise as possible, but no matter how hard I tried, I couldn't imitate Thomas's slow, falsely nonchalant step. I slipped on the rocks, ran into branches. Because of me, the whole forest knew we were there.

On our way back, our bags were still empty, and I felt that the situation was all my fault.

After hiking for more than five hours, we were nearing our camp when a partridge rose between the trees. Sure that I'd miss again, I glanced over at Thomas, who didn't budge. So I shouldered my Winchester and aimed, following a line ahead of the prey as it flew, then pulled the trigger. The shot rang in my ear, and the bullet caught the bird in full flight.

My pulse raced, but I stood stock-still, unable to move, the rifle still pointing at the spot where, just a moment ago, a partridge had flown. Thomas laid a hand on my shoulder. Then he went to fetch my trophy, a nice-sized catch, bigger than the ones we'd brought back on previous days. I felt the pride of an adolescent flooding through me. Which, after all, I still was.

We returned to our camp and prepared the game. This time, Thomas cooked it in boiling water.

"To switch things up," he said. "Here we often end up eating the same food."

I loved the smile that lit up his face, whose expression at times was austere.

"We'll be off tomorrow. We still have a good way to go."

I wondered how long the two of us would have stayed at the camp if I hadn't shot that partridge. As long as it took, I guess.

Under the moon's gaze, our bodies wrapped round each other, the echo of our pleasure was lost to the trees. That desire in my belly, in the caresses, never weakened. Even today, when I am an old woman, it lives on just as strongly inside me. Alone across from Pekuakami, when I close my eyes and breathe in the northeast wind as I do now, I can feel him in me. That flame is all that remains of him, and soon it too will die when I breathe my last, and that saddens me.

PASSES-DANGEREUSES

Every stroke of the paddle distanced me from one life and pulled me deeper into another. As someone who found it easy to talk, I was learning to listen to this world, both new and old, and become one with it.

Rivière Péribonka runs almost due north. The red and yellow leaves injected touches of colour into the screen of greenery that boxed the river in. As the temperature dropped, the water took on dark-blue hues.

Whenever Thomas noticed that I was tired, we'd stop for a day or two. I learned how to lay nets to catch fish, how to carry the canoe without injuring myself, how to walk without making a sound. Small step by small step, my body and spirit were adapting to the daily travel of nomadic existence. Over the days, the very idea of time became diffuse. But each morning, the increasingly cold bite to the air reminded us that we were nearing our goal.

We could hear Passes-Dangereuses long before we saw the falls. The echo of their roar, emerging from the earth's belly, reverberated through the mountains

and across the forest. The din grew increasingly powerful, and even metres away, we could feel the air become charged with the falls' exhalations and spray the surrounding vegetation.

Little by little, through the drizzle, the beast itself finally appeared. The dragon pounded the rocks with a howl of fury, leaving behind a frightening maelstrom.

An entire lake threw itself into the void with a blood-curdling roar.

"Aren't they beautiful?" Thomas had to shout.

"I...I don't know. More like terrifying."

"You've got to fear and respect the river's power."

Terror paralyzes, while fear leads to wisdom. That too I had to learn.

Thomas angled the canoe toward the bank.

"We'll sleep higher up, over there," he said, pointing at a small clearing on a rise. "Tomorrow, we'll start through the woods."

His voice betrayed a hint of excitement. We had reached the Siméons' territory.

That was our last night alone. At dawn, we would meet up with the rest of the family. Even though I was nervous and tired, the din from the falls kept me awake. I needed to feel his hands on me, his arms around me, his kisses banishing all worry.

I eased onto him to hear his heart beating between us. I kissed him, dug my fingers into his muscles, rolled my belly over his. He grabbed my hips and kissed my

preceding pages: Rivière Péribonka

38

eyelids. We lay locked together in the warmth of our shelter. Then he murmured, "*Tshishatshitin.*"

That was the first time anyone ever said to me "I love you."

TERRITORY

When we reached the winter camp, the men were off in the woods and the women were busy tanning a caribou hide. Set up at a distance from one another, the tents formed a hamlet perched on the top of a hill overlooking the lake.

Thomas's sisters, Christine and Marie, greeted us warmly. Marie served tea. Christine, who spoke a bit of French, sat next to me and asked how the trip had gone.

I tried as best as I could to describe the feeling of freedom that had washed over me the minute we set our canoe in the water. My sister-in-law saw the happiness on my face and in her brother's eyes. Love is something everyone understands, no matter the language in which it is expressed. Her warmth toward me eased my fears of being seen as a stranger intruding on a tight-knit clan. The fact that she and the others accepted me so easily showed just how open-minded the Siméons were. I hate to imagine the reaction of the inhabitants of Saint-Prime if Thomas and his long hair had swept into the life of the village.

While we spoke, Thomas began setting up our winter camp. He cut down several small fir trees, chopped off their foliage with his axe, then sharpened the ends to make poles.

When we'd finished our tea, Marie tugged on my sleeve for me to follow her. I sat between her and Christine in front of the caribou. They began by stripping the hide off the animal with a piece of flint, then hung it up. Afterward, with a moose rib and a great deal of patience, they continued scraping the hide until the fat permeated its tissues. Then they stretched it over a birch frame to dry. Lastly, they applied beaver fat and plunged the hide into boiling water.

For the tanning stage, my sisters-in-law built a fire into which they threw a wet stump and red pine bark so the thick smoke would waterproof the hide.

Watching them, I learned how to do it all myself. How many hides have I transformed over a lifetime? I couldn't say, but as I witnessed the slow, confident gestures of the Siméon sisters, I was being initiated like a child into age-old knowledge.

Before nightfall, Thomas had pitched the tent at a slight remove on a slope overlooking the lake.

"The best view," he said with a smile. Rectangular, high enough for us to stand up inside, it didn't seem much bigger than the kitchen in the house where I'd spent my childhood. On the ground, a carpet of fresh fir boughs filled the air with their perfume. In the centre, he had set up the stove we would use for both cooking and heat. But I didn't want to think too much about winter; it would be here soon enough.

We fell asleep in what would be our home for the coming months. One day, I would raise my children there and worry about them when the north wind blew and the snow threatened to bury us all alive. But that evening, our first night in the Péribonka, the only moment that counted was when I could feel my man's flesh quivering beneath my palms.

The next day, Thomas announced he was off to join his father and brother, who were hunting farther north. I felt a twinge of sorrow at the thought of being separated and would have liked to follow him. I always wanted to follow him. Still today I'd do the same, and his absence weighs heavily on me.

He left on foot that morning, carrying his gear, climbing a trail that led to the mountaintops. It was already cool outside. At this latitude, winter always seemed in a hurry to begin.

Marie, Christine, and I finished tanning the hides. While Marie made lunch, Christine pulled out her shotgun.

"Come on, let's go hunting."

I took the Winchester and some bullets and followed. Christine walked at the same slow pace as Thomas. People think that walking, like breathing, is the easiest thing to do. After all, it simply means putting one foot in front of the other. But in the woods, walking requires a great deal of skill since the slightest sound can frighten off any game. Over time, you learn where, how, and when to set your foot down, what rhythm to follow. Back then, even though I tried to disappear into nature, my lumbering step scared off the animals, and that made me furious. If I couldn't do something as basic as that, I would be of no use whatsoever.

My sister-in-law showed no sign of impatience. Her finger on the trigger, her senses on alert, her gaze dancing left to right, she continued walking at the same steady pace.

We came out at a lake on which a flock of wild geese had landed. We drew near. When the birds started to fret and grow restless, Christine took aim. I followed suit. She pulled the trigger, and so did I. The honking flock shot up, forming an immense and magnificent dome that darkened the sky. I quickly reloaded my Winchester, and just as I was about to pull the trigger again, Christine laid her hand on the barrel.

"We have enough for today."

The geese flew off, and their din gradually faded. My sister-in-law waded into the water and grabbed by the neck the three birds that floated there.

"You shot two," she said with a smile. "Who taught you to aim like an Innu?"

The blood dripping from the carcasses turned the surface of the lake red. Christine dropped the birds into a bag and pulled a pipe out of the pocket of her skirt, which she stuffed and lit.

"Do you want to try?"

I inhaled and the smoke invaded my lungs, choking me. I spat on the ground, hacking like a woman on her deathbed. Christine burst into her reedy, almost-childlike laugh.

In Saint-Prime, only men smoked. Every night after dinner, my uncle filled a pipe that he smoked sitting quietly in the living room. I never saw my aunt touch tobacco, and it would never have crossed my mind to try.

"You're not a real Innu yet after all, Manda."

She was about to retrieve her pipe, but I put it back between my lips and inhaled. As the taste of tobacco filled my mouth, my eyes began to water. I exhaled a white cloud, then handed the pipe to her. My sister-in-law responded with a knowing wink. It took all I had not to throw up on our way back.

That night I slept without Thomas. Where was he? Had he managed to kill anything? Was I in his thoughts as much as he haunted mine? I hoped so.

TRAPS

Marie and Christine spoke Innu-aimun to each other, and I could catch only snatches of their conversation. The words tumbled round in my head; it sounded like the two sisters kept repeating the same ones over and over and only the speed of delivery varied. Never mind, I liked being rocked by the lilting rhythm of a language that wouldn't let itself be tamed so easily.

"While Marie goes after the small game, you and I'll set a few traps."

I nodded. What did Christine think of the blond dreamer eyeing her? I have no idea, but I never felt her judging me. The fire crackled. The wind blew over the trees. I pulled my beret down low on my head, lifted the blanket back over my shoulders, held tight to the cup in my hands to take in some of its warmth, inhaled the perfume of the tea. A flock of wild geese could be heard off in the distance. Soon winter would descend on Passes-Dangereuses.

A few more weeks and thick snow would blanket the Péribonka, the whole territory in its icy grip.

Christine knew I was oblivious to all that awaited me, but she was kind enough to say nothing. I would find out for myself.

We began walking north to the mouth of a small stream. The creek ran deep in a valley ringed by tall mountains whose peaks were already white. Christine pulled out a trap. She set it, climbed onto the rocks, and reached out to lay it down on the moss, then set another one a bit farther along, also on a carpet of lichen.

To return, we followed the stream, walking alongside the forest. The setting sun slowly set the sky ablaze, and the cool of night spread over Nitassinan, sowing earthy fragrances. I have always loved that moment when light and dark come together, when time marks a pause.

We stepped up our pace. I had my Winchester and broke trail for us, on the lookout for any movement in the foliage. A partridge took off with a rustling of feathers. I raised my weapon, took aim and fired. Struck in mid-flight, it reared back, then crashed onto the rocks with a thud.

I gathered it up and held it out to Christine, who dropped the bird into the bag she'd used to carry the traps. I felt like giving voice to my pride, but we still had a long hike ahead of us, so we set off again.

"I was lucky. I didn't even think. I just fired."

Christine took a few seconds before replying. "There is no luck, Manda. The creature sacrifices its life. It is the one who decides. Not you. You must be grateful to it. That's all."

Thomas's sister's words got through to me and, little by little, guilt took pride's place. I gave thanks to the spirit of the creature whose inert body lay in Christine's bag. I hoped it could hear me.

By the time we reached camp, it was almost dark out. The men had returned, and as well as their hides, they'd brought back a moose they'd shot and cut into pieces to facilitate its transport, its meat already smoking over the fire. Some distance away, the dogs slept huddled together. Thomas folded me into his arms.

Marie roasted a section of moose, and the scent of grilled meat filled the air. In those days, we still didn't see many moose in the Péribonka. There were, however, lots of caribou. Although we didn't know why, *mush* gradually replaced *atuk*, and today the latter have almost disappeared from the region and are found only in the open country of the North.

We ate together round the fire, Thomas, his two sisters and his brother, their father—Malek—and I. The men talked about their trip, and I felt excited listening to their tale. I was determined not to be left behind to tend to the camp. I too wanted to head north, to hunt, trap, and see those far-off lands. Malek and his sons had brought back many beaver and mink pelts. The year was off to a good start.

After the meal, Thomas and I returned to our tent. I had missed the salty taste of his skin. And his gentleness, the power of his embrace.

We rose with the sun. A thick mist clinging to the crowns of the trees gave the entire valley an aura of mystery. But we had no time to reflect on it. We had to see to the moose, finish smoking the meat, tanning the hide. The two sisters had already begun the job. Christine asked me to check the traps for marten.

"If we've caught one, bring it back and set the trap again. Do you remember how?"

I wasn't sure, but I nodded anyway.

"Don't forget to set the traps on moss again. A marten is too intelligent to come out of the water onto rocks and leave tracks."

I nodded and left, a bag slung over my shoulder and carrying my shotgun. I took the same trail as the day before as far as the lake. The mist had lifted and the sun gave off a bright autumn light. The nip in the air gave me strength and courage. For the first time, I was alone in the woods.

I had no trouble finding the traps. There were two marten inside. Their curled-up bodies exposed their beautiful fur to the wind. I released them, then reset the traps just as Christine had shown me and headed back the way I'd come, scanning the edge of the woods. Not another animal appeared. We had enough to eat.

Back at the camp, the moose hide, scraped clean, now hung on a drying rack. Malek was making sinew for snowshoes. His two sons were busy chopping firewood. We would need a great deal for the winter. Everyone laboured, everyone had a task. I wasn't yet sure what mine was, so I began to prepare the marten as best as I could.

After a while, Christine came over to join me. She began removing the precious fur from one of the creatures with the confidence born of years of experience. Intent on my task, the time flew by. When we were done, we stretched the furs, then put them on the rack to dry as well. Christine smiled. Her way of congratulating me.

Marie had made supper. We ate outside in the autumn cool surrounded by the stillness of the forest. The moon climbed into the sky, spilling blue light onto the camp.

After dinner, Malek started telling stories of his youth. His tales revisited the family's past and that of the Innu of Pekuakami. Even though I couldn't catch every word, I let myself be rocked by the rhythm of the elder's tales. His frail, gentle voice expressed the resiliency and strength of those generations that had come before him and shared their knowledge and wisdom, as the others were doing to help me. I was part of this clan gathered round the fire beneath the moon reflected in the lake. Our full bellies and the hides and furs stretched out to dry told of a long, hard day's work.

Flames crackled. Christine laid something in my hand. I looked down at the object. She held out tobacco. I stuffed the pipe she'd offered me, lit it with a twig and inhaled. Malek's words soothed me. I pulled my beret down and laid my head on Thomas's shoulder.

Still today, nothing gives me as much comfort as the stories I'm sometimes asked to tell round a campfire. It is then that I experience the same sense of freedom that Malek's tales awakened in me that night. Some things change. Others stay the same. Which is as it should be.

NEEDLES

When I opened my eyes, Thomas was already gone. Day had barely broken, and the camp was silent. The scent of fir trees perfumed the air. That's one of the things I miss the most about nights spent in the tent, that fresh, tangy fragrance.

The boughs need replacing as they start to dry out; above all, never use spruce. I made that mistake once. I had gathered up a pile of branches and was trying, like Thomas, to interweave them so as to make a solid, compact mass. But the needles kept piercing my hands and knees.

Marie watched from a distance, laughing. My frustration grew, and after a while, seeing my wasted efforts, she came over and laid a fir and a spruce branch side by side. Comparing them, it was clear that spruce needles stick out all around the branch while fir needles lie flat. The former are prickly; the latter offer a smooth, silky surface. I was powerless to stop tears from welling up. My ignorance was there staring me in the face, and I felt foolish.

My sister-in-law patted my shoulder and began

removing the spruce boughs from the tent and replacing them with fir. She shook the branches until each found its spot as in a puzzle, gradually weaving a solid mat of greenery. There was no judgment implied in her attitude. I swallowed my tears and set to work at her side.

After that, I never needed help again. I also realized that handwringing is a luxury no one can afford in the forest.

I took one last deep breath of the sweet-smelling air, then got up. My sisters-in-law had made a fire round which they huddled as they drank hot tea to chase away the briskness of the morning air. The flame's reflection shone on their amber skin. Both had hale faces with harmonious features and the same intense gaze.

I poured myself some tea, which woke me up for good. I swallowed some dried meat, and we stayed put a bit longer listening as the forest came to life. Then we set to work. There was still meat to be smoked. And everything else to look after — hide, bones, fur.

INNU-AIMUN

The men hadn't returned from trapping, and we ate in Marie's tent every night. After the meal, we lingered, smoking our pipes. My sisters-in-law conversed in what was still for me an incomprehensible song of which I'd grasp no more than a word or an expression here and there. The language raised a barrier around me, and it took me a while to free myself of it.

Innu-aimun is not an easy language to learn. It has only eight consonants, seven vowels, and fifteen distinct sounds, so the inflexion given to a term can change the meaning in a subtle or profound way. There is no written form, no linguist to analyze meaning. No feminine or masculine. There is only animate and inanimate. At first, I stumbled constantly and made no headway no matter how hard I tried. Eventually, I understood that it is not just a different language from French but a different way of communicating. It's a language whose form is adapted to a world in which the hunt and the seasons dictate the pace of life. The order of the words is not as important as it is in French. And the order varies depending on the circumstances.

Kun, snow, becomes *ushashush* when it is "light snow," *nekauakun* for "grainy snow," or *kassuauan* when speaking of "wet snow."

The language is under threat today because, for Innu-aimun to be spoken properly, it needs to be learned on the land. Today, young people prefer the French they're taught in school. Those youngsters grow up blind to their past, orphans of their origins. But who is interested in all that nowadays? Other than old holdouts like me who see the past as the only treasure?

*

Heavy snowflakes fell slowly from the sky as though hesitating. Winter announced its arrival at an unhurried pace. Confronted with nature so pure and untamed, I felt miniscule and yet increasingly as though I'd found my place.

I stood watching the snow fall on the still-sleeping forest when Christine got up. I served her some tea, and then, as we did every morning, we headed out to check the snares. My sister-in-law tied the metal wires and hid them so as not to give away their presence. Above all, she touched none of the trails the hares had made. That morning, we found two in the traps. The day was off to a good start.

*

The daily chores — trapping, hunting, harvesting, and smoking the animals' meat, preserving their hides — filled our days. But in the evening, when I returned to the solitude of my bed, I increasingly missed Thomas's hands, his caress, his breath on my neck. I had only known him for a few months and already his absence was hard to bear. When he finally showed up with his father and brother, loaded down with pelts, I told him that next time we would leave together.

"We'll see, Almanda."

"No, it's been decided, Thomas."

He smiled to see me so stubborn. "It's tough up there. You have to walk a long way. You have to be quick at preparing the hides."

"I know that. Do you think we sit twiddling our thumbs here in camp? We work as hard as you do, I'll have you know. I didn't follow you here to live apart from you. Next time, we're going together. Period."

He shook his head. It was his way of giving in. Laughing, I threw my arms around him. I dug my fingers into his hair, clawed his skin as though I needed to prove to myself that it was all real.

THE SACRED MOUNTAIN

Two weeks later, dense white magma blanketed the Péribonka. The snow erased its rough edges, turning it monochrome.

In Saint-Prime, winter inspired dread. People shut themselves up in their cabins until springtime, living off the stores put aside over the harvest period. Winter was a trial to be got through.

For the Innu, winter simply represents one stage in the year's cycle. Cold bites into flesh and freezes waterways. Snow complicates travel. At the same time, it is an ally to hunters, who can easily follow prey that has suddenly become more vulnerable.

And so I faced the first winter in the Péribonka with a combination of dread and excitement. Malek gifted me with a light pair of snowshoes perfectly suited to my weight that he had made out of spruce and woven with sinew. His gesture touched me. Although the elder proved to be even more reserved than his sons, the language barrier didn't stop us from liking each other.

Malek was the first to bear the Siméon name. Until then, the family's name had been Atuk. But the priests didn't like words they didn't understand, so they forced the Innu to adopt French surnames. Thus, the Atuk clan became the Siméon family. Malek was born in Pessamit on the North Shore. One day, when he and I were alone together, he told me how he had ended up in the Péribonka.

This was before farmers had settled the shores of Pekuakami. The only whites there were the employees of the fur trading posts—Tadoussac's was the first, but the Hudson Bay Company established several others afterward.

Just as Malek turned eighteen, famine struck.

"The animals avoided us. Reduced to licking resin off the underside of the bark of fir trees, many children died of hunger. It was a period of great distress."

"What about the elders? How did they explain the catastrophe?"

"Even they didn't understand," he told me. "No one had ever seen anything quite like it. We must have failed to respect the Supreme Being. Someone had provoked His wrath and we were all paying the price."

Malek interspersed his tales with long pauses, as though delving further ino his memories each time. He drew deeply on his pipe, then resumed his story.

"Rather than die of hunger, I decided to leave Pessamit. I paddled upriver heading north. But I could barely kill enough game to survive. Starving and exhausted, I carried on, alone in the silence of the forest, and as I advanced, nature folded in on itself like someone curling up into a ball to resist the cold. The trees grew smaller and their rock-hard trunks became almost impossible to chop with an axe.

"By the time the first cold struck, I had passed Lac Plétipi. From there on in, rivers flow to the northwest. I had arrived at Nitassinan's boundary and was about to enter Cree territory. For the first time in my life, I was a stranger.

"When winter truly set in, I reached the spot where the forest and the world I knew ended. Before me, stretched out as far as the eye could see, was the white expanse of the far North. I pitched my tent in that desert. If I died, no one would ever know. If I survived, it would be because the Supreme Being had decided it should be so. Having come to the end of the trail and of my strength, I put myself in His hands.

"I had just enough wood to keep warm and not much food. Sometimes, fierce storms forced me to take refuge in my tent for days at a time, listening to the wind's fury. Alone in the blizzard, I prayed for salvation for me and my loved ones.

"Time and space blurred. My senses grew more sluggish as my strength abandoned me. I was ready to accept my fate.

"Then, one morning when the cold was so intense that a thin layer of frost had crystallized on top of the snow, the ground began to shake. A dull roar sounded, and my tent quivered like a leaf in the wind. I grabbed my rifle and ran outside. The stark light blinded me. Then, little by little, an endless moving forest appeared before me.

"My grandfather had told me of *atuk*, the rulers of the open country of the North. But I had never before seen the great herd, or so many living beings gathered together in the same spot. *Atuk* was fleeing the polar cold of the Arctic winter. The animals advanced crowded together, and I watched as they passed before me. One old male fell back. I took aim and fired. *Atuk* dropped to the ground as the tide of his fellow creatures moved on. I thanked him for making the journey here so I could survive. I now had enough meat to last me till spring. *Atuk* had saved my life.

"As the days went by, the wind's bite lessened and the weather grew warmer. I left before the snow became too soft for my snowshoes. I found my canoe where I had left it. I pitched my tent by the river. Now I had to wait for the spring thaw.

"Once the current had borne the ice away, rather than paddle back down toward Pessamit, I followed a small river that flowed west. Crossing a lake, in the distance I caught sight of a colossus unlike anything I had ever imagined. Amid those isolated mountains, a granite giant brushed up against the clouds. I headed toward it and, once there, began to climb. The higher I climbed the scarcer the vegetation became. Soon I was walking on bare rock, oblivious to the wind, the cold, and the sun. Sweat trickled down the nape of my neck, the cold turned the skin of my face to glass. Despite the pain, a feeling of peace washed over me as I gained altitude. I felt neither fatigue, nor hunger nor the bite of the wind.

That stark mountain harboured a magic inside that touched whoever had the courage to approach.

"From the summit, I saw all of Nitassinan laid out at my feet. Alone between land and sky, I saw the place I had come from and the place I would go. Night had fallen by the time I returned to my tent. Stretched out on my bed of boughs, I could hear the wind whistling at the top of the sacred mountain. In the morning, I gathered up my belongings. Several waterways have the Otish mountains as their source. Some flow west to the lands of the Cree and the Inuit. Others flow south to the territory of the Innu.

"I chose the transparent waters of a small river running southwest. Soon I was paddling again surrounded by forest, following the liquid path that ran between imposing treetops.

"As the weather grew warmer, game became more plentiful and I no longer felt I had to hurry. On the shores of a great lake, I came across an old man and his wife who had wintered there. They were the first humans I had laid eyes on since the previous fall, and they were surprised to see a hunter arriving from the North. The man asked where I had come from.

"'I'm from Pessamit, but I left my territory a long time ago. To be honest, I don't really know where I am now.' The old man fixed me for a moment with his placid gaze.

"'You wintered up there?'

"'Yes. I saw the flat, open expanse and the great herd of caribou. And mountains with bare peaks.'

"'You were lucky that wasn't the last thing you

saw…All alone up there at your age…It isn't safe. The winter is merciless.'

"His wife watched us from a distance. Seeing my drawn features and how thin I was, the old hunter took pity on me. 'I killed a woodland caribou yesterday. There are a lot of them around this spring. A good thing. You'll eat with us.'

"I thanked him for his hospitality.

"The evening was unusually mild, and we ate outside by the fire as if it was summer. The woman served me blueberries in bear fat. Something my *kukum* used to make. My hosts were discreet and reserved. The man told me we were on Lac Péribonka and that the river that had brought me here bore the same name.

"'It flows as far as Pekuakami,' he told me. 'That's where the Ilnuatsh spend the summer.'

"I had heard the elders speak of the Innu lake on the western boundary of Nitassinan.

"'Given its size, I thought this lake was Pekuakami.'

"The woman, who had yet to say a word, looked up and smiled. 'When you see Pekuakami, you'll understand.'

"I woke up the next morning at daybreak. The old man had already left to check his snares. I thanked the woman. She waved goodbye, then returned to her task.

"I loaded my bags into the canoe, not knowing what lay ahead. Before me, the lake stretched as far as the eye could see. To the east and the west, deep bays penetrated the woods. The old man had pointed out the portage to bypass the impassable waterfalls, and I set off.

"I had been gone from my village for nearly a year. I had known hunger and exhaustion. This trip to the borders of Nitassinan had led me to the river whose current now bore me away.

"After two weeks, around a bend, behind some sand dunes, the lake appeared. I had reached my journey's end."

And so, Malek and I had the shared experience of discovering a new world when we were roughly the same age. Thomas and the others had spent their lives travelling up and down Rivière Péribonka. But for the old man and me, the river had swept into our lives and left a mark on each of us.

As his life hung in the balance, driven by an almost mystical faith, Malek had chosen to follow his destiny, convinced it would guide him. *Atuk* had shown him the way.

As for me, it was a young man's eyes meeting mine that had prompted me to leave everything behind, and like Malek, I eventually found my way.

I believe this is why Malek always felt a certain fondness for me. We came from different worlds, but the same desire for freedom had led us to the Péribonka.

THE GREAT HUNT

Thomas asked me to gather my belongings.

"Where are we going?"

"Up north. We leave tomorrow."

I felt a twinge of excitement in my belly. He too hated the long separations. I packed our bags and our provisions for the trip. Christine was somewhat worried.

"It's hard up there, Manda. There's no rush. You've got lots of time to go."

"Thanks for your concern, Christine. I want to know everything. Thomas will look after me. I trust him."

"Me too, Manda. But I'm afraid that he's so attached to you it will cloud his judgment."

With hindsight, I understand her reservations. I still had everything to learn.

We started out at dawn. In the cold, the forest looked petrified. Snow crunched beneath our snowshoes. We looped around two mountains and the sun showed itself above their peaks. We headed north along a small winding river that was bordered by tall fir trees with white, heavy arms. We advanced at a good pace, stopping only for a quick lunch. Thomas broke trail through the snow, and I followed in his footsteps. The sun gilded our faces.

"How're you holding up, Almanda?"

"I'm not even tired. I'll have you know that I'm tough, plus I'm younger than you!"

We were carefree. "Foolhardy," my sister-in-law would have added. "Happy," we would have replied.

When he made my snowshoes, Malek had taken my height and weight into account, and I was able to follow Thomas without any difficulty. Night falls quickly at that latitude, and we pitched our tent as soon as the sun began to set. Thomas chose a snowy bank sheltered from the wind by tall trees. Once he had the tent up, he used the axe to chop a hole in the river ice and dropped a few fishing lines in the water. After a meal of dried meat, we lay down, snuggled together by the stove. Only the sound of our breathing broke the silence of the northern night.

The following morning, Thomas went out early and returned with two walleyes. I had the fire going by then, and we ate the fresh fish with relish. We walked in much the same way for five days before setting up camp next to a lake ringed by hills, where we stayed put for two weeks. We caught an abundance of marten, mink, and even lynx. We ate the meat, then dried the hides. Next, we travelled westward, this time camping deep in the woods.

The mercury dropped, and the wind blew night

and day. We had several streams nearby, and I helped Thomas with the traps and snares. It was cold, of course, but we lacked for nothing.

A week later, we moved a day's walk away, to a flatter area where the snow was not as deep. We laid our traps by a wide river, but since game was scarce, we moved on. And so, for a month, we tracked fur-bearing animals. The hides piled up, and our load grew increasingly heavy to pull, making each new move a chore.

The ongoing quest held an element of excitement. It's hard to know whether a given place will offer good trapping. You have to try your luck and hope. Over the weeks spent hunting with Thomas, I learned to conserve my energy and set various kinds of traps. We lived symbiotically and, every evening, ended up back together in the tent. There was a sort of innocence in that love, which did nothing to stop it from enduring.

After five weeks, having harvested enough hides, all dried and carefully preserved, we finally returned to base camp. Malek's shining eyes were a gift. His approval meant a great deal to the huntress I was becoming. Marie made a meal of *mush*, and we all dug in hungrily. The hunting season was off to a good start.

From time to time, I would still think about my aunt and uncle. At any given hour of the day, wherever I was, whatever I was doing, I knew where they would be and what they'd be doing. By choosing a life out on the land, I had chosen freedom. Of course, it came at a cost and involved responsibilities toward the members of my clan. But at last I felt like I was living without chains.

THE TRIP BACK

Wherever it exists, spring is welcomed by humans. After months without light, they feel as though they've been reborn.

With the return of milder weather, Saint-Prime would liven up. On Sundays at mass, the women would sport their new dresses. The men would trade in their beaver hats for felt headgear. At church, during his homilies, the priest would urge his flock to pray twice as hard for their future crops now that work on the farm could finally resume.

For the Ilnuatsh, spring was a time of excitement as well. After living in isolation on their hunting grounds, families readied themselves for the return to Pointe-Bleue. The time for reunions was fast approaching.

Game became scarce now that the heavier snow made it difficult for the animals to be out and about and everyone was in a hurry to leave. But they had to wait for the ice to free the rivers. The journey took several days to organize. Certain things would be left behind. Large tents, snowshoes, and other objects that wouldn't be needed during the summer months were stored in raised shelters to keep them safe.

We had amassed a fine harvest of hides, and this contributed to the good cheer that reigned in the family. For my part, I was torn between sadness at leaving the Péribonka, where I'd spent such happy months, and excitement at the prospect of embarking on another long journey.

For Thomas and the others, the trip to Pekuakami was of a solemn nature. It announced their having come full circle.

We set out before dawn in the bluish light of the full moon. As well as his canoe, Thomas carried a large bag strapped to his shoulders with leather ties. My own bag was heavy, and I struggled to make headway. Malek pulled the sled, overflowing with our cache of furs. Absorbed in our tasks, we advanced in silence. The sun still shone when we finally reached Rivière Péribonka.

The river was still iced over, and we had to wait there for several days. When the current finally carried off the ice with a huge crash, we were ready. Behind us the waterfalls thundered as the rapids quickly bore us away. The canoes sliced through the waves, which broke against the birchbark, splashing our faces. The wind danced in our hair and a heady joy flooded through us.

Several months earlier, I would have been terrified to find myself surrounded by a churning mass of water in a frail craft weighed down by all the gear we had piled inside. But Rivière Péribonka was no enemy. It was an ally waltzing us back to Pekuakami.

MANOUANE FORKS

Swollen by the spring runoff, Rivière Péribonka looked markedly different from what I had seen the previous fall. The rushing waters had become torrents through which our small floating caravan had to manoeuvre with care. From the back, Thomas guided our canoe with a sure hand while I kept its bow in the centre of the V that formed in the eddies. When the waves knocked us about too much, it was of the utmost importance not to hang on to the sides of the canoe since that would have tipped it over immediately. We had to raise our arms instead, holding the paddle above our shoulders to stabilize the boat.

Sometimes, the canoe took a plunge and the river seemed about to swallow us whole. Each time, I felt my heart skip a beat. But the craft righted itself and continued on its way over the exuberant waves. The sound as they splashed against the hull was like a hand beating a drum accompanying our dance across the water.

It took us only seven days to reach the mouth of Rivière Manouane. Later I would explore that magnificent body of water and the path it cuts through vertiginous cliffs of black granite to reach a beautiful lake ringed by green hills. We called the spot Manouane Forks, where several families stopped off for a few days or even a few weeks.

"We'll rest here for a bit," Malek decreed.

We pitched our tent on a spit of sand at a remove from the others. It was the first time I had seen so many Innu gathered together in the same place outside of Pointe-Bleue. After months of isolation on the land, it felt good to be part of the small village of tents. People laughed and children ran and played together. I recognized a few faces encountered the summer before. Some had attended our wedding and seemed happy to see me again. The warmth of the reunion had special meaning for me, given that my blond hair and blue eyes reminded everyone of my origins.

Over the months, I had worked hard to learn Innu-aimun and now could make myself more or less understood. Thomas and his family knew how difficult it was for me and made an effort to speak slowly. But in the festive atmosphere at Manouane Forks, people spoke much too quickly for me to grasp everything. When I lost the thread of a conversation, I'd just laugh. All Innu understand laughter.

Each evening, everyone gathered round a bonfire. An elder brought out his drum and sounded the beat. The dance could begin.

At my aunt's house, dancing was thought to involve a dangerous element, something to be wary of. But the Innu believe that dance soothes the souls of animals and expresses the love we all feel for one another.

The dancers followed the beat of the drum. They moved with a slow, bouncing step round the flames that made faces glow. I watched, fascinated. I had never seen so many men and women engaged in the same pursuit. Christine must have noticed because she grabbed me by the arm and pulled me into the circle of women. The men, including Thomas, formed their own circle and the two groups turned like the sun.

The only one singing, the elder with the drum, used his voice at times to guide them. Every once in a while, one of the men would cry, "Hey!" Or a dancer would turn and pull a face at the man or woman behind them to make them laugh. Some kept their hands close to their chests; others let their arms swing with each step.

The light of the full moon was subdued, and the songs of the Innu disappeared into the forest of shadows. The cold had finally eased its grip, and the dancing round the fire warmed both hearts and bodies.

Back in our tent, Thomas pushed me onto our mat. He removed my clothes one by one, sometimes taking his time, sometimes in a hurry. His hands slid over my hips, kneaded my belly, my breasts. His palms burned my skin. I took his face between my hands, kissed him with parted lips. When I close my eyes, that intoxication inhabits me still. No one, not even death itself, can take that from me.

After several weeks, we struck camp and continued on our way. As we advanced, the landscape softened. The forest took on hues of lighter green. We could feel the lake nearby and so we paddled even harder.

Pekuakami appeared round a bend, huge and commanding. After months spent in the forest, we were blinded by the light of its infinite horizon.

Happiness is something that is hard to define. But happiness is what I felt at that moment, in the canoe I shared with Thomas, surrounded by our people, looking out onto the lake. Our lake. We glided across it in silence, too moved to speak. Other caravans bobbed ahead of us and behind us. The long journey of the Innu was nearing its end.

As we passed next to Rivière à la Chasse, I pictured Thomas paddling up it to see me again. I glanced over at him. He smiled. My aunt and uncle would be working in the fields at that time of day. June is a crucial month for farmers. Seeds begin to sprout. The men break their backs working, praying to Heaven for sunshine or rain.

In Pointe-Bleue, the village seemed just as I had left it at the end of last summer but different too. Yet I felt like I was coming home.

We pitched our tent at the foot of the hill, by the church, on the spot where I would have my house built later on.

THE HUDSON BAY STORE

The day after we arrived, I went with Thomas and his father to the Hudson Bay store to sell our hides. It was a log building off the trail, located next to the lake to accommodate canoes. Inside, the fragrance of spices and smoked hides held sway. The shelves were laden with merchandise of all kinds: clothing, flour, animal fat, dishes.

Surly and a fierce haggler, the manager, Tommy Ross, was a former *coureur des bois*. I often fought with him and his sidekick, Skeen, over a fair price for our precious furs. I too knew how to be inflexible.

Ross seemed impressed by the quantity and quality of what we had to offer. After a lengthy discussion, he agreed to pay us 110 dollars, a considerable amount at the time. I had never seen that many bills in my life. The summer could begin.

Every day, new families arrived and pitched their tents. They sold their hides to Tommy Ross and bought supplies in his store. Those whose hunt had been less successful the year before had to pay back the debt they'd contracted the previous fall. The

Hudson Bay man gave easy credit, knowing full well that those who owed him money would be paying him back with interest the following spring.

After months of austerity on the land, the money burned a hole in the pocket of many Innu, who spent it freely. The women bought themselves elegant dresses; the men, suits they wore with strange top or bowler hats. Ross sold them all kinds of more-or-less useful items and quickly recouped the bills he had handed over. Having lived on a farm, where we counted every penny, I found all the spending frivolous. Even Thomas, usually so careful and wise, spent more than seemed reasonable to me.

I hesitated to raise the issue with him or even with my sisters-in-law, for fear of vexing them. One day when the two of us were alone, I confided in Malek, knowing the older man wouldn't judge me.

"Why is everyone just throwing their money away?"

He looked at me with his beautiful, faded-brown eyes. "Throwing it away?"

"All the stuff people buy, frilly dresses and hats, it's ridiculous. It's wasteful. Why not put at least a bit of it aside?"

He shook his head. "What good is money on the land?"

"It's no good, of course, but we might need it later. You never know when you might have a bad hunting season. A bit of a cushion could come in handy."

"Who knows if we'll be back? We could decide to go somewhere else next summer. Pessamit, for example. Or Essipit. Or even Uashat Mak Mani-Utenam. A beautiful spot. In that case, what would be the use of your money if you left it here?"

"But Malek..."

"In a few weeks' time," he continued, "we'll all return to our hunting grounds. Whatever is most precious to an Innu, Almanda, he must be able to take with him."

The next day when Thomas, who was heading out to the Hudson Bay store, asked me what I would like, I said: books. My husband, who didn't know how to read or write, seemed disconcerted.

"I was thinking of a dress or a necklace. A parasol maybe?"

"I'd like to take books up there with me this fall."

There were no books on Tommy Ross's shelves. We had to canoe to Roberval. I came back with several novels and a bible.

MOURNING DOVES

A fortnight after our arrival in Pointe-Bleue, one breezeless morning Thomas and I went to visit my aunt and uncle. The sun rose and gradually chased away the mist that clung to the banks. We paddled up Rivière à la Chasse, which flowed between the slopes of tall grasses. This place where I had grown up seemed to me now both familiar and strange.

From afar, I recognized the hillock where we put our cows out to pasture. We left the canoe on the dark sand and began walking. In the fields, animals grazed steadily. Behind a pretty grove of birches, the house with its wood siding painted white came into view. It seemed smaller than I remembered it.

My uncle was busy chopping wood, and the sharp sound of the metal as it split the logs echoed in the warm air. So intent was he on his task, his brow covered in sweat, it took him a while to notice the presence of visitors on his property. There were so few visitors. When he finally caught sight of us, he hesitated for a second, probably wondering what the two Indians wanted. But suddenly his features lit up. I had rarely seen him smile, and it warmed my heart. He called for my aunt, waving her over.

"Thérèse, come see who's come to visit!"

A small woman stepped out onto the porch, frail in her grey cotton dress. Despite the distance, I could see her squinting as she scanned the horizon.

"Almanda? Is that you?"

I waved to her in answer, and she raised her arms toward the sky. She and my uncle embraced me.

I had often felt I was a burden for them and that they had taken me in out of Christian charity, driven by religious conviction. I was touched by the obvious joy they expressed at the sight of me. They were the only family I had known before I met Thomas.

We drank tea on the porch, surrounded by the fields that for so long had been my entire world. My aunt plied me with questions. And she listened carefully to every answer.

"I prayed so hard for you this winter. I was worried. If you're happy over there, Almanda, that's all that matters, my child."

"Don't worry, ma tante. We're happy, we have everything we need. You know how I could never stay put. I was always up for a trip to the village to run errands or to help uncle chop wood."

She nodded with a smile.

"Well, I've got what I wanted, ma tante."

She laughed along with me. We ate her cabbage soup to which she'd added a bit of lard. She gave me news of the village. Plans to build the church were progressing. Some villagers, my uncle included, thought it was too great an expense. But the priest said it would attract parishioners to Saint-Prime.

Many settlers would, indeed, end up living there, not because of the church, but because of the region's abundant resources. On that day, as we listened to the melancholic cooing of mourning doves pecking patiently in the grass, all that seemed far away.

We left after lunch. My uncle and aunt kissed me goodbye. He went back to his field, and she watched us go. What was in her heart in that moment? Did she suspect we would never see each other again? Illness carried her away the following winter. Her health had never been sound, and the demands of farm life had worn her out. My uncle, shattered, lived alone for a few years, toiling away from dawn to dusk on his plot of land.

It was the priest, worried when he didn't show up for mass two weeks in a row, who found him dead in his armchair by the wood stove. His funeral was held in the newly inaugurated church.

THE WEDDING

Summer for the farmers meant a period of hard labour. For the Innu, however, after months of living in the cold and the snow, it was a time to be carefree. It was also the season for weddings.

Over the winter, Marie had met a young man whose territory was at the north end of Lac Manouane and had spent several weeks hunting with him and his brothers in the Péribonka. We were overjoyed when they announced their upcoming union, even though it meant our clan would lose one of its members. Although she didn't let it show, Christine took the news hard. The two sisters had always been inseparable.

We celebrated the wedding that summer. A sweat-lodge was built for the occasion, a simple hut made of willow branches tied together with hides spread out on the ground. We lit a fire inside and entrusted it for four days and nights to a keeper.

At the end of those four days, the tent was ready. All the loved ones, me included, gathered round the fire. The firekeeper threw onto the burning stones a concoction whose principal ingredient was cedar, and dense smoke filled the hut. It was dark inside, and the heat was almost unbearable. The air burned our lungs and stung our eyes. My head started spinning, and I clutched on to Thomas so as not to fall.

Later, when I was better prepared, I could appreciate the power of the shaking tents and, in moments of doubt or anger, often sought refuge there. But that first time, if it hadn't been for the reassuring presence of Thomas and the others, I would have bolted. Inside the smoke-filled hut, time and space commingled, and my mind drifted among the shadows.

When we finally left the hut, Marie stayed inside. She spent the whole night there while her future husband slept in another tent.

The next day, a large crowd gathered round the future spouses.

Just as Thomas and I had done the year before, the two took turns smoking the pipe. White plumes rose to the sky, toward the one I called God and Thomas called the Supreme Being. They spoke their vows in front of everyone and were served a cedar brew in a double-coned vase. Afterward, we all danced round a bonfire overlooking the lake. Marie, usually so reserved, couldn't stop smiling. Her happiness was wonderful to behold.

The celebration lasted till late into the night, and by the time I went to bed I was exhausted. So was Thomas, who fell asleep the minute he laid his head on my shoulder.

I lay awake in the darkness, rocked by the slow

rhythm of his breathing. My sister-in-law's marriage reminded me of my own and how much my life had changed. It took my breath away, and I pressed up against him.

STORYTELLING

Reading is one of the rare activities from my old life
that I did not give up. In the house where I spent my
childhood, despite the starkness of our surroundings,
books played an important role.

There was a bible, of course. I read it so often that
I still know whole sections off by heart. When I was
little, the Old Testament fed my desire for adventure. Abraham, the battle between David and Goliath,
the prophets' mystical tales, Exodus—each of those
stories evoked a mysterious and exotic world. I dreamt
of seeing the desert, the Dead Sea, the Jordan River,
the pharaoh, and Moses parting the waters of the
Red Sea.

My aunt also had novels, which she kept out of
sight in a small wooden cabinet, and which I read several times over. Our schoolteacher, a young woman
with a lively, independent mind, noticed my love of
reading and lent me as many books as I wanted. And
so, even though we lived on a backroad of the colony,
books nourished my curiosity from my earliest days.

The stories of Tshakapesh, Aiashess, and any tale

featuring Kuekuatsheu (Wolverine) as told by the elders plunged me into the same dream state as books did. However, having grown up with the latter, I couldn't imagine life without them.

That first winter, I brought along ten novels. A book for each month spent on the land. That's not bad considering all the necessities we had to transport. As we left, Thomas put the books in his bag and he was the one who carried them.

Mostly, I read at night in the tent by the light of a candle. Once I had our children, Thomas's absences were made easier because of those books. I would read them out loud to our little ones.

One day, my eldest daughter, Anne-Marie, who must have been five at the time, interrupted me as I was reading her *The Count of Monte Cristo*.

"Why are you doing that, Maman?"

"Doing what, my child?"

"Why do you need that," she asked, pointing at the book, "to tell a story?"

She stared at me with her big eyes.

"Don't you like stories, Anne-Marie?"

"Yes, Maman. Especially the one about Kuekuatsheu. He's funny. But I don't always get your stories. And they aren't funny."

I drew her to me and held her close. Our tales, relayed through word of mouth, tell the story of the land and of all the creatures that live there. The story I had been reading conjured up a continent and a world she knew nothing about. Anne-Marie, born and raised in the Péribonka, knew nothing of counts and their battles. Was I wrong to insist on introducing my children to a world so foreign to them? I stroked her jet-coloured hair and took her face between my hands to draw her closer.

"You know, Anne-Marie, they are only stories. How we tell them doesn't really matter. Books have their own way of speaking. You must listen to them too."

She studied me, her uncertain gaze searching mine.

"Okay, Maman."

My daughter laid her head on my chest, and I picked up where I had left off.

None of my children has inherited my love of books. But they all know how to read. Their own children went to school. And some of my great-grandchildren are now in university.

Sometimes, it can take a while to harvest the fruit of a tree. It can even take a lifetime.

THE CANOE ROLL

As summer drew to a close, Malek was the one who would decide when to leave for the Péribonka. As soon as our baggage was ready, he'd stand before Pekuakami every morning, scanning the horizon, looking for signs in the clouds and the sky.

The elder was afraid of threatening shifts in the lake's mood, which could strike without warning. Even today, large ships remain docked during bad weather. He would tell us to set out only when he was sure we'd have good weather all the way to the mouth of the river. The elders knew how to read the sky like a book. That fall, Malek didn't like what he saw. After watching the lake with his faded gaze, he'd return in silence to his tent.

Days passed and the weather didn't improve. The whole family was impatient to be off, of course, especially since it would be foolhardy to leave too late. Frost arrives early in Passes-Dangereuses, and when ice forms up north, the river ferries blocks of ice that could slice through a canoe.

After three weeks of waiting, Malek didn't feel any

more reassured, but time was short and eventually we had to start off under a menacing sky. We paddled at a good clip, but scarcely two days later the northeast wind awoke. It whipped up the lake, forcing us to find shelter. Pushed by the wind, a pelting rain fell in bursts, and huge waves crashed onto the shore with a roar. There was nothing to do but wait. Malek hid his concern as best as he could, but he grew increasingly worried with each passing day.

At last, one morning a red sun rose above the lake. We slid our canoes into the water without taking time for breakfast. We paddled twice as hard and sweat ran down our brows. When we finally caught sight of the mouth of the river, daylight was fading. Fatigue had started to set in, yet our journey had just begun.

I was only sixteen, but I had the pride of a centenarian, so I refused to complain. The portages were tough, especially because I hadn't yet developed the roll of flesh that forms on the neck where the canoe's crossbar rests and that serves as a cushion. At that time, every Innu had a canoe roll. It did eventually form on my neck after a few years and it is still there almost a hundred years later, encrusted under my skin. But at the time, the boat left my back black and blue and, despite the pain, I refused any help from the others.

Days passed and the weather remained stormy. The dark sky spat cold rain and the wind slowed the canoes' progress. Sometimes, the raging river forced us to seek shelter along its banks since Malek was afraid the water would drench our stores of flour and sugar. Despite our best efforts, we fell farther and farther behind. Worry took hold of the whole group now. The cold had become biting, and we had to bring out warmer clothes. Even the wild geese passed high overhead without stopping. They too were in a hurry.

There was no good fishing to be had. The year before, Thomas and I couldn't eat everything we'd caught on the way north. We had even smoked part of our catch to keep it from spoiling, while this fall, without fresh fish we were forced to dip into our winter stores of biscuits and lard.

I was perplexed by the turn the situation had taken. This region I had discovered, eyes and heart open wide, only a few months earlier, now showed me its dark side. The beauty of the landscapes was still just as breathtaking. I marvelled at the vertiginous granite cliffs that touched the clouds and the dense forest that crowded the river and its limpid waters.

A violent storm forced us to spend a week inside our tents, shaken by icy gusts. Waves as big as Pekuakami's swells rolled over the raging surface of the river. We couldn't move or even hunt. Once more, we were forced to wait even though our time was already running short.

One night, the wind died down. In the morning, fine snow shrouded the Péribonka in white. Winter had arrived. We set our course for Passes-Dangereuses. The canoes advanced beneath a milky sky. Single-minded, Thomas scanned the surface of the river. Ignoring the danger, we picked up our pace, paddled harder, walked faster. Snowflakes died on our brows, and despite the cold, perspiration trickled down our necks.

We paddled into the dark under a sickly moon whose pale light disappeared in the inky water. I felt neither fatigue nor my sores nor my aching muscles. No one said a word, all our energy was focused on the effort it took to make our way upriver. At last, Malek guided his canoe to a small beach sheltered from the wind. We would spend the night there.

We pulled the canoes onto the sand without bothering to unload them. While Christine started the fire, I made tea and set out a few biscuits and lard for everyone. The men made quick work of pitching the tents, and we sat round the flames, hides on our shoulders to warm us up. In the distance, we could hear the roar of the river. Tomorrow would be a tough day. We went to bed the minute we'd wolfed down our supper. Thomas held me tight. The heat of his body penetrated mine. Suddenly, the forest seemed hostile.

By morning, the clouds had disappeared and it had stopped snowing. The cold bit into our faces and the canoes had trouble ploughing through the waves.

We unloaded some of the bags, which Christine and I carried on our backs while the men, leaning far out over their poles, pushed the canoes against the current with all their strength. There was a kilometre of white water before the rapids began. At the foot of a huge waterfall, we pulled the canoes up onto the sand.

Already exhausted, we were about to tackle one of the most difficult portages. We would have to scale a mountain up a steep cliff along a narrow trail carved into the rock. Knowing that many people had gone before us gave me the strength to ignore the perspiration stinging my eyes and the fatigue in my arms and legs. Once we crossed the mountain, we had to set down our bags and return for the canoes and the remaining gear. It took us two days in all.

Just as we were about to slide the canoes back into the water, bad weather forced us to delay further. From inside our tents, we could hear a cold rain that the northeast wind turned to ice on the canvas walls. Fear crept over us.

We were stuck there for a week. The dampness cut us to the bone and it was impossible to get warm.

When we were finally able to set out, a thin sheet of ice covered the river's edge. We had to navigate between the icy patches floating on the water, advancing cautiously just when we should have been racing forward. Sitting at the front of the canoe, I paddled, focused on the water's surface. From time to time, a block of ice grazed up against our craft and we held our breath. I was beginning to think we would never make it to our destination.

One evening, off in the distance I heard a thundering unlike any other and I felt immense relief. Malek's smile had returned. Once again he had managed, despite great challenges, to guide his people to their territory.

TOBOGGANS

Barely a week after we arrived, an unusually violent storm swept across the Péribonka. Mighty gusts battered the forest with a roar. Trees, shaken like fescue, snapped everywhere. We could see neither earth nor sky. Confined once again to our tents, which shook in the squalls, we were forced to dip into our winter stores.

Despite the persistent bad weather, Thomas refused to allow discouragement to set in. "We have no say in the weather, Almanda."

"I know, but it still worries me. We're not in Saint-Prime. If we run out of butter, we can't just borrow some from the neighbour."

Thomas laughed. His laughter was spontaneous and it relaxed his handsome, occasionally earnest features. "We could," he said.

"Don't you dare make fun of me, Thomas Siméon."

"It's true."

I glared at him.

"We're not all alone, Almanda. Joe Fontaine's family is camped on the other side of the mountain. The Moars a bit farther south. At the end of the small river at the foot of the rise, the trail leads to Jean Raphaël's territory and, farther down, to Paul-Émile Gill and his wife, Madeleine. If we need help, we'll find it."

He was right, because the isolation we lived in was relative. Other families were camped nearby, and in the event we needed something, they could help us out. Unless their reserves were as low as our own, a possibility I chose not to think about.

*

The next day when I opened my eyes, a strange calm reigned over the camp. The sun shone. Nature seemed frozen under a thick white mantle.

Thomas had left. I put water on to boil and had a look around. The branches of the pine trees bowed under the weight of the snow. It was as though the forest held its breath. The tracks from Thomas's snowshoes disappeared into the woods. While everybody slept, he had headed out to lay snares, bent on replenishing our supplies.

I made tea. I sipped it slowly, and its heat spread through my belly. The climb had left its mark on me—my eyes were itchy, my joints were sore, and I felt all-embracing fatigue. I hadn't yet achieved the level of endurance the others had, and although I did my best to hide it, every action required slightly more effort of me than it did for them.

Thomas returned just as I was on the verge of setting out. He shook the snow off his shoulders. Seeing that I carried my Winchester, he drew me to him.

"Stay. You're allowed to rest, Almanda."

"I'll rest once I've brought back my share of game."

I donned my snowshoes and followed Thomas's tracks, curious to see where he had laid his snares. Then I climbed a tall hill, weaving through the spruce trees that grew in tight rows. Under clear skies, the summit offered a panoramic view. I waited, my senses on high alert. However, seeing no sign of life, I began my descent via the north slope. My shotgun on my shoulder, I advanced slowly through the trees. I had begun to lose hope when a large partridge flew straight for me. I fired and a second later, it fell to the snow.

I gathered it up, gave thanks, and put it in my bag. I walked north for another hour with no more sightings before I headed back, skirting the hill from the west. When I finally reached the camp, I was starving. Thomas was waiting for me.

"You were gone a long time."

"Not that long."

I showed him the partridge.

"At least you brought something back," he said. "Malek and Daniel didn't shoot a thing."

Our bad luck persisted. Over the next days, every morning I'd walk through the forest checking the snares. But more often than not, I returned empty-handed. Malek said it reminded him of the year of famine he'd experienced in Pessamit.

Thomas and his brother decided to head north. Despite my insistence, he refused to let me go along.

"We're off to the other side of Rivière Péribonka

and the mountains to the east, Almanda. You're a good shot, the others will need you here."

Hoping to return with a good haul of pelts and meat, they decided to take the bare minimum for baggage, leaving behind even the travel tent. They left with one toboggan each on what promised to be a tough trip. With a heavy heart, I watched them disappear, following the little river that would lead them to Lac Péribonka. The route exposed them to the wind, but it was faster, allowing them to head straight north toward Lac Onistagan. They would then cut across the mountains to reach Lac Manouane and its dozens of small bays where they would be sheltered from the wind as they hunted.

Time passed and our traps caught very little. For days in a row, we had no meat. The cold intensified, and at night, despite the thick furs piled on top of me, I couldn't get warm.

We had no news of Thomas and his brother for a month and a half. Every morning when I woke up, I hoped to see them. I made tea and breakfasted alone in the tent before heading out with my Winchester to check my snares.

Christine and Malek had no more luck than I did.

At night, often unable to sleep, I would spend hours reading by the flickering light of a candle. Reading helped me to cope with Thomas's absence, but without him the tent seemed so very empty.

THE REUNION

Thomas, his brother, and the two dogs returned via the river, both men and dogs pulling their share. From afar, the dogs had caught the scent of the camp. I ran to Thomas and hugged him close. I breathed in the fragrance of spruce on his skin, plunged my fingers into his thick hair. Fatigue ravaged his handsome features.

Malek inspected their heavy load, stroking the pelts to evaluate their worth. The hunt had been bountiful. Thomas and Daniel also brought back two caribou, which they had cut up into pieces, removing any bones to facilitate transportation. It made for a great deal of meat. We would have enough to eat over the coming weeks. It must have been heavy going towing such a load through the mountains to our camp.

The two brothers had sheltered in birchbark huts or simply slept under the cover of tall fir trees, covering dozens of kilometres in the cold and snow as they tracked game that had fled the Péribonka. And they had returned with a fine collection of pelts as well as food for the whole family. When the brothers were little, that had been Malek's job. Now his sons had taken over, and the old man made no secret of his pride.

Christine set about preparing the hares we had left for supper while I helped Thomas and Daniel untie the bags and store the hides. Tommy Ross would give us a good price for them when we returned to Pointe-Bleue.

We ate together in the tent, the scent of grilled meat mingling with that of fir boughs. Thomas and his brother told us about their long journey. They had come up against violent winds that slowed them down. The deep snow made walking difficult. For three weeks, they didn't see a single animal. Only when they arrived north of Lac Manouane did their luck finally turn.

"We trapped beaver and lynx. Fine specimens. Once we had enough, we decided to come back. When we arrived at Lac Péribonka, we saw caribou. We managed to kill two. We couldn't have transported more, anyway. We carved them up on the spot. The dogs had a feast."

The two animals, who had pulled more than their share, were asleep, curled up outside the entrance to the tent. Daniel ate without looking up. Exhaustion furrowed his features.

"The trip down from the lake was tough going," he said, "since a good two feet of snow had fallen three days earlier. The toboggans kept sinking, so we had to take breaks."

"A good thing Daniel's as strong as a bear," Thomas added with a laugh.

At last, his brother smiled. Like Thomas and his father, he was a tireless hunter.

"You should have seen the load he had to pull," Thomas continued, looking over at Malek. "On top of which, he made it look easy."

In response to a playful shove on the shoulder from his older brother, Daniel gave another faint smile, almost despite himself.

"Daniel's a good hunter," Malek said. "He's just like my father, who once killed a bear with nothing but a crooked knife. The animal appeared out of nowhere while we were tanning hides. It's rare for them to attack humans. It must have either been starving or crazed. My father rolled round on the ground with it. My mother, who'd always had a fear of bears, couldn't stop screaming. When he finally got up, covered in blood, *mashk* was dead. Daniel's like him, strong and silent."

Malek looked at his son and, for once, Daniel Siméon's smile was so wide we could see his teeth.

"Tomorrow we'll take some meat to Paul-Émile Gill," Christine announced. "The old man is all alone with his wife, Madeleine. He didn't sell many hides last spring and wouldn't have brought much in the way of reserves for the winter. And he's no longer of an age to travel as far as Lac Manouane. I'll go there tomorrow with Almanda, father."

Malek nodded.

After the meal, I followed Christine and we put

together the bundle. She laid almost a third of the caribou meat aside for the old man and his wife. Seeing my surprise, my sister-in-law explained, "They won't make it through the winter otherwise. They have no children and are all alone there. Sometimes they don't even return to Pointe-Bleue in the summer because they're afraid they won't be able to make it back in the fall. The hunting hasn't been good this year, but at least we can make do, Almanda. Unlike them."

THE NASKAPI WOMAN

The next morning, Christine and I set out early with one of the dogs. Christine had divided the meat among three toboggans, one pulled by the dog and the other two by us. In all, there was more than half a caribou.

The Gills lived on the other side of a small mountain, and it was a good three-hour hike to reach them. We found the old man making snowshoes by the fire while his wife chopped firewood. Their camp was well organized and included a large tent for shelter, a more modest tent where they stored their gear, a smoke-house set back in a clearing, and a food cache.

Christine waved, and the old man nodded while his wife put water on to boil. The sun warmed our faces. Christine and I helped the elder lay the meat away with the rest of his stores. Then we sat outside to drink our tea.

Paul-Émile Gill was a small man with deep-set eyes in an emaciated face. He wore a woolen cap pulled down low on his skull and seemed lost in his bulky clothing, but he radiated the confidence of a man in his element. Rotund, her face a patchwork of a thousand lines and wrinkles, his wife's eyes sparkled. She had been a beauty in her youth, you could tell. She did all the talking while her husband, for the most part, simply nodded or shook his head to show whether he agreed or disagreed.

They hadn't had much luck hunting either. They weren't planning to return to Pointe-Bleue in the spring, his wife said in a voice at once soft and high-pitched. She offered us bannock with blueberry jam. We stayed for an hour talking to the Gills in their camp. Madame Gill spoke Innu with an accent I had trouble placing.

When we stood up to leave, they thanked us warmly. The sun was still high in the sky. A gentle breeze wafted between the trees. Although winter in the woods can often seem harsh, sometimes it offers up the gift of golden days when light dances across the snow and warms both body and soul.

"You noticed her accent, hey?"

I couldn't hide anything from Christine.

"Yes, it did strike me."

"She's Naskapi, that's why. She comes from Ungava, northeast of the Otish mountains. She and her husband never had children. Old man Gill was a great hunter. My father still talks about him with admiration. He does pretty well considering his age."

So there was a woman in the Péribonka who came from even farther away than I did. That made me smile.

BEFORE

It's not easy to describe the territory as it was before. The woods before the clearcut. Rivière Péribonka before the dams.

You have to imagine a forest spilling from one mountain to another and on beyond the horizon, and visualize that same sea of vegetation tousled by the wind, warmed by the sun. A world where life and death battled for supremacy, and at its centre, between sandy banks or austere cliffs, a river as great as those that flow into the ocean.

It's hard to describe because it no longer exists. Paper mills have devoured the forest. Rivière Péribonka has been sullied and subjugated. First by the log drive, then by the dams that swallowed up its unbridled falls and created reservoirs whose water now feeds power plants.

Passes-Dangereuses, where my children were born, where I raised my family and where Thomas and I so often made love, have disappeared, engulfed by tons of water. A sort of Innu Atlantis, a place that exists only in the memories of old people like me and will disappear with us for good. Soon. Like the portage trails patiently blazed by generations of nomads. All that knowledge will vanish from the memories in which it lives on still.

All that is left is Pekuakami. Our young people see it, breathe in its scent, hear its song. They fish for ouananiche and walleye there. They appreciate its long beaches carved up by rocks. The lake continues to elicit wonder with its size and its beauty, and thanks to it, Nitassinan remains real for them and for me as well.

But our territory beyond the lake lives on in our hearts. One day, we will see it again.

ALONE IN THE WORLD

The cold did not loosen its grip and, although we had enough reserves to hold us over till spring, we needed more hides. Thomas and Daniel embarked on two other expeditions to Lac Onistagan. Seeing my man leave was always heartbreaking. No matter how hard I tried to reason with myself, it didn't help.

"Give it time," he'd always say when I pleaded to go with him. "It's tough. Next winter we'll go, at our own pace."

He was right, except that I hated living apart from him. Just as I hated the thought of having to stay behind, which most of the other women accepted. Maybe it was because I grew up with the aching feeling of being abandoned by my birth parents. Many orphans experience the same profound emptiness.

My aunt and uncle, who had no children of their own, had taken me in because they saw it as their duty. I was adopted out of Christian charity—no more, no less—by very pious people who made sure I wanted for nothing. And although they learned to love me, I was never awash in the tenderness that calms children's fears.

Thomas changed all that. From the very start, I could tell that I mattered to him. From the very start, I loved him as much as he loved me. I realize in hindsight that it was a mad, irrational love. I don't regret following my heart.

I was a young woman in a hurry, but Thomas knew that a certain amount of knowledge is required to get by in the forest. By staying in the camp, I could learn from Malek, just as his children had before me. The natural order had to be respected.

Malek laid his traps, and I accompanied him every day. He never spoke while in the forest. That world held no secrets for him, although he would deny it. "No one ever knows everything about it, Manda. I learn something new every day."

I was the one who was learning at his side. How to place the trap downwind watching the movement of the surrounding branches, or how to wait for the right time of day before going out in order to take advantage of the best weather conditions. Learning all the little details, each one of which was important.

Christine was just as patient with me when it came to the other daily tasks in the forest, some of which bumped up against my impetuous temperament. Tanning hides was a long and fastidious task, and I often became discouraged, convinced that we would never see the end of it. Christine knew how to reassure me.

"Go make us some tea, Manda, while I finish this bit," she'd say, her voice as gentle as snow falling on a windless day. "A cup of tea will do us good."

I went to boil the water and prepare the infusions. We took a break sitting by the fire. Then we returned to our chore. Learning perseverance is a lengthy process. They must have loved me very much—me, almost an adult!—to take the time to educate me. Because that is what they did. It didn't matter that I knew how to read, write, and calculate better than they did; I was still unschooled there.

Over the days, weeks, and years, my knowledge grew. Christine loved making everyday objects out of birchbark. We'd often work on them together. Bark can be gathered in spring or autumn when the sap rises or falls. The older the tree, the thicker its bark.

For baskets, Christine preferred fat, mature trunks with a thick skin. First we placed the bark under a weight to flatten it. The grey surface had to be scraped carefully away with a knife. Once the piece was the shape we wanted, we sewed the ends together with spruce roots, then sealed the container with spruce resin to make it waterproof. We added pretty decorative patterns by biting the bark.

The final product is light and strong. I still make the same baskets and sell them in the craft store. Tourists love them. In their eyes, they are just knick-knacks, souvenirs. But for me, they are a way of keeping the past alive. When I work with bark, I am with Christine once again, sitting by the warmth of the fire as we work silently. When I tan a hide, I do as she taught me. I go through the same motions and, as long as I do this, she, Malek, and all the others will still be here with me.

THE SUGARING-OFF

"We'll be making snow candy, so we'll need big baskets."

Thomas, his brother, and his father had laid large strips of bark down on the snow in front of Christine and me. I didn't know what the men meant. Christine took my arm.

"Come give me a hand."

We set to work, and as we made the baskets, my sister-in-law explained the meaning of snow candy, a delightful term I had never heard before.

It took us several days to finish. The sun set late, which made our task easier. For each basket, Malek cut little boards out of pieces of wood. Then, with an axe, he cut slits into the trunks of the maple trees round the camp. When he felt the notch was deep enough, he inserted one of the small boards inside and sat a basket on top. In next to no time, the translucent sap began to flow, dripping into our birchbark recipients. Twice a day, we had to empty the precious liquid into large pots, straining it through cotton fabric to remove any impurities.

Thomas and Daniel built a frame out of spruce trunks on which they hung the pots full of maple water, and we lit a big fire below.

The sap began to simmer, then boil. Just when the liquid looked like it was about to overflow, Christine thrust a fir bough inside the pot. Should the level of water get too low, we'd transfer it into another pot, until there was only one pot left on the fire containing all the boiled-down concentrate from the maple water.

It took us all day. As it boiled down, the liquid took on a pretty amber colour and the sweet smell of sugar wafted through the camp. From time to time, Christine rolled a bit of syrup round a stick, then unrolled it onto the snow to check its consistency. Near the end, she added a bit of moose marrow. "To give it more taste," she said. Then, satisfied with the result, she removed the pot from the flames. The taffy was ready.

Everyone gathered round. Christine poured strips of syrup onto the snow, and they solidified in the cold. I had never tasted anything like it; the others must have noticed because they smiled as they watched me eat.

Every culture has its own rites. But regardless of skin colour or origin, the act of eating is an opportunity for people to gather together and share.

Christine laid down the strips of liquid magic extracted from a tree. In Innu hands, it turned into maple-flavoured honey. When we were almost done, Christine vigorously stirred what was left of the syrup until it began to crystallize and form a light brown granular substance that she poured into small baskets. We would have enough sugar till the following winter.

When I had my own family, I made winter candy every time the weather made it possible. It took long warm days and cold nights for the sap to flow freely enough. The children helped, and it became a favourite family activity, especially since it meant that spring was on its way and we would soon be returning to the lake. The young ones chopped wood to feed the flames, helped collect water, and amused themselves chasing away any overly curious squirrels that might tip over the baskets at the foot of the trees.

I have memories of smiling faces, shining eyes round the fire, and bursts of laughter. Life in the forest could be demanding, but its every pleasure seemed magnified tenfold.

No one at home makes snow candy anymore. We buy maple syrup and maple sugar at the market. It's good, but not as good as the kind that we made together.

END-OF-YEAR CELEBRATIONS

My first five years in the Péribonka taught me how to live according to the rhythm of the hunting seasons. Some seasons were good, others were harder.

I accompanied Thomas, and Daniel too at times, on the great hunt. We either followed Rivière Péribonka down to Manouane Forks or up toward Lac Onistagan. Once, while tracking caribou, we walked as far as the Otish mountains. I saw the mountain Malek had described. Bald and austere, it dominates the North, and the Creator's presence can be felt in those sacred places.

I loved the demanding nomadic life, with the frequent need to set up and dismantle camp, never really settling in comfortably. A storm could confine you in your tents for great stretches of time. However, the lifestyle gave me the sense of freedom I had dreamt of since childhood.

We travelled a great deal, but no matter where we were, we always returned to Passes-Dangereuses for Christmas. Several families, relatives and friends of the Siméons, came together there for the holidays. In any event, in late December and January, it was so cold the animals didn't leave their shelters. We all met up on the banks of Rivière Péribonka, bearing an abundance of food, dried meat, bear fat, cranberries—favourites of Malek's and the other elders—flour for bread, and tobacco, of course.

Malek was bent on us always being the first ones there. I think it was a matter of pride for him. We pitched our tent and chopped wood as we waited. When the other families arrived, we helped them set up their camp. While the children played, the adults made meals together.

The year after her wedding, Marie showed up unexpectedly with her new husband. Her surprise visit warmed our hearts, and Christine flew into her arms. It had taken them a good while to come all the way from Lac Manouane. I suspect that Marie was suffering from a bit of homesickness and that, even though she got along well with her in-laws, she missed Passes-Dangereuses.

On Christmas Eve, we all crowded together into a large tent. At midnight, one of the men shot his rifle into the sky. Then we prayed and sang. I had been raised to respect religion and found the Innu to be a very pious people. We prayed the rosary. There was something beautiful and moving in gathering round the same fire, in communion with God and nature.

Old Joe Fontaine told the nativity story, and everyone listened attentively. He was originally from the North Shore, and I had trouble understanding his accent. The language spoken by the Innu of that region is purer than the speech of the Ilnuatsh who live on the territorial boundary of the Naskapi and Cree, whose influence can be heard. They also kept in touch with the Wendat to the south and the Mohawk, who, it is said, travelled as far as Tadoussac in the old days. Malek had told me those stories that went back before my time.

Between Christmas and New Year's, people didn't do much hunting, but I still went out almost every day with my shotgun since it's something I've always loved to do. The others played cards, checkers, or smoked as they drank tea round the fire while the children played a cup-and-ball game made of fir boughs or ran all over the camp.

The men organized contests of skill and strength, and everyone watched, urging on the participants. Marie's husband won the strength tournament, which consisted in breaking a bone from a beaver leg. The bone is short and doesn't offer much in the way of a grip, so it truly requires great strength to break it. My sister-in-law was visibly proud when it snapped, and everyone applauded her husband's prowess.

Some of the competitions took place outdoors. Thomas entered the snowshoe race, and I ran in a race in which we wore mocassins without snowshoes. It was fun, and the crowd laughed loudly at the poor contestants' desperate attempts to avoid sinking up to their waists in the snow, wriggling like caterpillars to make any headway.

Neither of us won, but we had a good laugh, especially at my attempt. I don't quite know how I managed it, but just when I thought I'd reached a firm patch of snow, it collapsed under my weight and I somersaulted, ending up with my head stuck in the snow, to the general delight of the spectators. Unable to get up on my own, I had to wait for someone to come to my rescue.

No medals were awarded and they weren't actual competitions, but we did have lots of fun. That lightheartedness in the depths of winter did us good.

At day's end, everyone gathered round the elders to hear their traditional Innu stories. Crowded together in rows, children and adults listened closely. That was where I first heard the story of Mishtamishk, the great beaver; and Mishtapeu, the giant; and the horrific Atshen. The one to be avoided at all costs. Several of the elders claimed to have spotted tracks belonging to that cruel and evil being. Atshen was the only figure in the woods that the Innu feared because his violent nature was incomprehensible to them. Even today, there are those who don't dare speak his name and who believe the forest landscape bears traces of his passing.

The storytellers also recounted the adventures of Tshikapesh, who has the power to change his size at will. Many stories revolve around him.

I loved listening to those epic tales since they helped me understand both nature and the world. The characters could be either funny or frightening, and the stories often changed depending on the person who told them.

Today, I'm the elder of the community and I know all the stories of the supernatural. But unfortunately, on the reserve our heroes' adventures are of little interest to our young people and the world they describe is no longer their world.

On New Year's Day, as on Christmas Eve, a shot was fired into the sky at midnight to greet the new year and thank the one drawing to a close. It was my favourite time. Everyone outdid themselves cooking food to share and bring pleasure to the others. We all worked together, and each family made its contribution. That year, Christine and I prepared the cranberries in bear fat that Malek loved so much.

The children received gifts their parents had made for them—dolls, snowshoes, little sleds. Everyone ate at the same time. Some issued a challenge—for instance, who could drink the most cups of bear fat, a feat I never dared attempt.

After the meal, the elders brought out the drum. Considered sacred because its vibrations allowed communication with the animal spirit, it was reserved for the wisest and for the shamans, who used it to chase away bad spirits. On New Year's day, it lent its rhythm to our hearts and our chants, which rose up to heaven and the Creator above. Such was our belief.

The next day, the celebrations were over and everyone had a heavy heart. The time had come to go our separate ways and repair to the winter camp. Each family would return to its splendid winter solitude.

BEADS

Those years of our youth sealed the feelings Thomas and I had for each other. Over time, our passion became an enduring love. I was grateful to him for accepting me as I was. It had required a certain open-mindedness on his part, something not everyone possessed.

Over time, the forest transformed my body. The sun weathered my pale skin. With all the portages, my muscles grew strong and I became more resistant to the cold; I learned to ignore the insect bites and to put up with hunger if necessary. Whenever I struck a match on my skirt and lit the tobacco in my pipe, no one doubted I was Innu.

At the end of our fifth winter, as we travelled back to Pekuakami, my belly grew hard and began to swell. I said nothing to Thomas, but when he saw my rounded abdomen, he looked at me wide-eyed. He had been awaiting this pregnancy for a long time.

Our harvest had been plentiful, and during the trip back we added three beautiful bear skins. Our bags were heavy, but the being growing inside me increased my strength tenfold. I could walk longer, lift heavier bags.

At Pointe-Bleue, we saw Marie again. The hunting had been poor on Lac Manouane. Fortunately, we had enough hides for everyone.

Marie, who already had two children, was pregnant as well. The next year, at around the same date, we would return from Passes-Dangereuses and Lac Manouane with new babies. The family's future seemed assured.

I did a great deal of beading with my sisters-in-law that summer. We made caps. Almost all the women wore them back then, and I never saw my sisters-in-law without theirs. Generally red and navy blue or black, they were decorated with pretty glass beading. It takes a good week to make each hat. But the result is magnificent.

Malek explained to me that women used to make beads out of bones, shells, and stones such as agate. Glass beads made our task easier, but the work still required a great deal of patience and attention to detail.

Christine and Marie taught me to shape elegant curves that gave a flow to the fabric. I liked playing with the colours too.

Even now, at night, despite my gnarled fingers, I like sitting in front of a hot wood stove beading clothing, jewellery, and the small objects that we used back then and which we sell to the craft store now. All First Peoples do beadwork. The techniques vary for each nation, as do the patterns and choices of dye:

But the principle, shared by the women of an entire continent, is the same.

I taught my daughters to bead as well. We'd sit together, and the youngest would sort the beads and pick up the ones that fell to the ground. The girls would make tea and a snack. Each of them contributed and learned as they watched the more experienced among us, just as I had done with Marie and Christine.

The two sisters, who were only a year apart and could easily be mistaken for twins because they looked so much alike, always worked together. They set to work in the morning, placing a large plate with hundreds of multicoloured beads in front of them, and didn't stop until evening. By their side, I learned how to line up the beads and play with blues, reds, yellows, greens, blacks. I made many mistakes and often had to start over, but over time I managed to keep up with my sisters-in-law, sitting with them round their large dish with its rainbow contents, beading in silence.

The summer of my first pregnancy, we made clothes for the coming babies, and Christine helped us decorate them. We had to work quickly since the days were growing shorter and so we worked twice as hard.

When the time came to leave, everything was ready. Marie and her husband set out for Lac Manouane, and a few days later, we left for Passes-Dangereuses. The trip went well. A month later, we were at our camp. Luckily, my pregnancy was already well along.

I didn't accompany Thomas and his brother on their hunting expeditions, but stayed behind with

Malek and Christine. I had no idea how things would unfold. I let myself be swept along by events.

When I finally went into labour and my contractions grew closer together, a midwife came to our camp. Christine helped her. Thomas was there to welcome our baby as she emerged from my womb, and he washed her and laid her on my chest. The newborn nestled in instinctively. I listened to her breathing and tried to feel the beating of her little heart against mine. The smell of blood mixed with the fragrance of pine, and my damp hair stuck to my cheeks. I had never felt so weary in my life.

Yet I would have taken on Atshen himself to ensure my little girl lacked for nothing. I promised her she would never be alone the way I had been. Christine smiled and squeezed my hand in hers. She understood how I, the orphan, felt on the birth of my first child.

It was dark outside when Christine went back to her own tent. Thomas fed wood into the stove and spread a bearskin over our daughter and me. Then he sat close by, watching over us. It was the first time I ever saw him cry.

ANNE-MARIE

Anne-Marie had inherited her father's almond eyes,
his brown skin as velvet as the moss on rocks, and his
vanilla scent. She observed the world with curiosity.
I loved her more than anything as soon as Thomas
laid her in my arms and I heard her breathing inside
the warmth of the tent.

The whole clan had been preparing for her arrival.
Malek had made a small hammock that he hung from
two posts, with a thick mat of fir boughs underneath
to cushion her fall should the hammock tip. Christine
had made her winter clothing that she'd lined with
rabbit, careful to place the fur on the inside next to
the child's skin. Thomas had made a harness so that
I could carry her around with me.

The arrival of a baby changed the way our whole
group functioned. I could no longer accompany
Thomas, and his absence weighed heavily on me. Up
until then, life in the woods had meaning only if I was
with him. Now there was my daughter too. I took her
everywhere, even hunting. The outings did me good.

Mostly she slept strapped to my back, rocked by the rhythm of my snowshoes sinking into the snow. She didn't cry often; she took in her surroundings with an eagerness that pleased me. The sound of gunshot didn't frighten her, and we lived fused to each other. You don't learn how to become a mother. You get by the best you can.

We weren't on our own. Christine and Malek always gave me a hand. But every evening, my daughter and I ended up alone together in the tent.

Whenever Thomas returned, he spent a great deal of time with Anne-Marie. His face, which was usually so serious, shone during those times. He could spend hours with her, and it was obvious how much he too minded being away. One can learn to live apart, but the heartache is still there.

In the spring, Anne-Marie underwent her first journey to Pekuakami. We placed her in the middle of the canoe, and the caution with which Thomas handled the boat had to be seen to be believed. Sometimes I teased him about being a father hen.

"We can go faster, you know. Just because she's a girl doesn't mean we have to go at a snail's pace."

He simply scowled at me, which made me laugh. At Manouane Forks, we stopped to see Marie, who had also given birth to a daughter. My sister-in-law and I sat with the others round the campfire at night nursing our babies. Now that I had given birth to a child of the forest, I felt even more at home, more Innu, if such a thing was possible. The birth of my first daughter erased any lingering doubts I had, and after that no one ever alluded to my origins. For all of them and for me, the matter was settled.

I got pregnant again that summer, and this time round things were more difficult. I felt nauseous and dizzy. The others looked after both me and Anne-Marie when I was unable to.

In March, the midwife returned to Passes-Dangereuses. The baby refused to leave the womb. I screamed in pain, drenched in sweat. Christine mopped my brow. I was in labour for forty hours. When Thomas finally laid Ernest on my chest, I hadn't even enough energy left to smile. The little one latched onto my breast greedily, and I fainted.

After a few days spent regaining my strength, I was able to get up. I stayed inside in the warmth of the tent. Little by little, I recovered. Ernest was a big, beautiful, plump-cheeked baby with eyes as black as the depths of the lake. He looked at me with an intensity I found troubling. As if he wanted to make sure to remember me. Even when I cuddled him and held him tight, he kept on staring. Perhaps he sensed that our days together were numbered.

Two weeks after his birth, I found him one morning stiff in his hammock. I felt as if my chest had been ripped open, and a sudden cold sliced through me as though the wind had whisked away the tent, subjecting me to the northeast gusts. A cry rose from deep inside, the lament of a wounded she-wolf. I howled into the wind, half-crazed. Everyone came running. Christine took me in her arms, trying to calm me, while Thomas stared at his lifeless son. Afterward, a vast silence fell. It was so heavy that our shoulders sagged and our backs bowed under the weight of it.

It was my first contact with death, the first time it had shown me its hideous face.

We buried Ernest at the foot of a maple tree. Thomas laid him deep in the hole, placed stones on his body, and Daniel shovelled earth into the grave. For years, I went to pray at the foot of the tree where my baby lay. I had chosen that particular maple because it was tall, beautiful, and strong, and I thought it would protect my son. But the loggers chopped it down with all the others to feed their forest-devouring beasts. Then they built the dam. Today, Ernest sleeps beneath that wasteland engulfed by icy water. My little one. My darling.

My third pregnancy was difficult as well, and I spent all those months studying my belly. No matter how much Christine tried to reassure me, I was afraid that whatever had caused Ernest's death was inside me. During those dark months, only Anne-Marie's smiling face enabled me to keep the faith.

The midwife was unable to come because of the weather, and Jeannette was born in the middle of a storm. It was Christine who helped deliver her. The wind's howls covered my own, and all around us the forest creaked. Then, from my womb emerged a baby with large, dark, frightened eyes. Thomas laid her on my chest and for a second I hesitated. He steered the baby toward my breast. The little girl began to nurse. I could no longer hear the raging storm; the tent was filled with the sound of a suckling newborn. Suddenly, everything seemed normal again.

For weeks, I coddled that child, scrutinizing her every move. I worried every time she grimaced and rushed over as soon as she started to cry. But days went by and Jeannette grew stronger. She babbled for hours at a time in her hammock, grabbed my breast as I fed her as though she wanted to make the milk flow more quickly. Jeannette was hungry for life. After several weeks, I understood that all would be well.

I experienced motherhood as a great responsibility entrusted to me. Life on the land could appear fragile, and it often was. Humans' survival depended on their ability to adapt to the world, to live in harmony with nature, like the other species do. We had our place. This is the way I came to understand our forest existence.

The Creator gave me a large family. Those children were the fruit of the love between Thomas and me, the child from nowhere, and I did everything I could to keep that magic alive. Anne-Marie, Jeannette, Antonio, Clément, Virginie, Laurette, Gérard, and Gertrude grew up in the Péribonka. Each new child became a member of the group. The eldest looked after the youngest, and as with everything else, the work and responsibilities were shared. That was a great help to me since I could never have raised such a big family on my own.

Inside the tent, I devoted a few hours every day to teaching the children to read and count. Then, during the summer, the children could attend classes at Pointe-Bleue. I managed to teach enough grammar for them to be able to write, and enough arithmetic for them to solve simple problems. But I knew it wasn't enough for a useful education. For that, my children would need to go to school. The thought broke my heart.

THE CABIN

Anne-Marie was twelve and Jeannette nine when I decided to broach my plan with Thomas. When I'd finished, he took a sip of tea without looking up.

"I'm serious."

I struck a match on my skirt and inhaled the tang of tobacco from my pipe.

"I want Jeannette to go to school."

Thomas knew what that meant. I continued, "We can't spare Anne-Marie up north, I know that, so we'll send Jeannette. Anne-Marie will go next year. That way, we'll have enough helpers. Afterward, it will be the others' turn."

Thomas stared at me, and both of us sat unmoving for a moment. Then I added, "We'll have to build a house in Pointe-Bleue for the winter."

He was no longer the young man I had known. His features were more chiselled now, but his eyes still shone just as brightly. "All right, Almanda, we'll do that."

Sending Jeannette to school meant I would have to stay behind in Pointe-Bleue with the children during the winter. It meant a lengthy separation. We both knew this.

That evening, while the little ones slept, we made love quietly. How would I manage to spend all those months away from him?

*

In the spring, we received a tidy sum for our hides, even though the manager tried to argue that there had been a drop in demand for beaver. Then I went to Roberval's sawmill. I knew the boss, William Girard, a little since he came to Pointe-Bleue from time to time to buy crafts, which he then sold in the south.

Everyone called him Gros Bill because he was a huge fellow with a belly so prominent it cast a shadow before him. The children called him *mashk* (bear). Jovial by nature, he took everything in stride.

I found him in his handkerchief-sized office at the back of a lumber yard that had all kinds of boards, planks, and beams so neatly stored that I was impressed. The smell of fresh pine filled my nostrils, and I could picture myself in the middle of a forest. Gros Bill was busy writing and he took a while to notice me.

"Madame Siméon? To what do I owe the honour of your visit?"

He straightened up in his chair, and I thought the buttons of his shirt would pop off. Gros Bill smiled. He had eyes that sparkled.

"I want to build myself a cabin for the winter."

He frowned. "A house or a cabin?"

"A small house, Bill. My second eldest starts school this winter. We're going to stay on in Pointe-Bleue."

"That's a good idea, Madame Siméon. The little ones need their schooling."

He clapped his huge hands together, and the noise gave me a start. Gros Bill laughed. "How would you like to proceed?"

I knew nothing about boards or wood panels and even less about building a house. As on many other occasions, I decided to trust myself and my own judgment.

"I've got three hundred dollars, Gros Bill. You'll give me credit for another three hundred dollars' worth of material. With six hundred dollars, I should be able to have something built. I don't want your top quality. I just want a small, sturdy house."

"I see," he said in his deep voice. "Madame Siméon, you'll need boards. And two-by-fours to assemble the structure. You can insulate it with sawdust. It will keep you warm and doesn't cost much. With that, you'll be set for the winter."

Unlike the manager at the Hudson Bay store, Gros Bill had an honest look that made me trust him. We came to an agreement.

I needed authorization from the band council to have a plot of land granted to me on the reserve. I explained to the chief that I didn't have the money for either the land or a permit. I wouldn't be able to manage otherwise. He assured me he'd speak to the councillors. He called a meeting and together they approved my request, all except an old Innu named Paul Natipi, whom everyone knew as Tambush.

"They're not from here, they come from Pessamit. They've got no business to be building something in Pointe-Bleue," he declared.

The chief argued and the other council members were on my side, but Tambush would hear none of it. "They've got no right. Let them build their house in Pessamit."

The council adjourned without having reached an agreement. I was devastated. If they turned down my request, how would I send my children to school? There was no way we could spend the winter in the tent on the edge of the lake. The wind was too fierce, it would be unbearable. Should I camp in the woods? It made no sense. The situation seemed so unfair.

Thomas tried to reason with Tambush. After all, even though Malek had been born in Pessamit, Thomas had been born here. His sisters and his brother had always lived in the community.

For three days, I had no news. Then the chief dropped by. His long white hair fell over his shoulders and gave his features a certain nobility.

"You can build yourself something, Manda. Tambush finally listened to reason. You can't hold it against him. Some people forget that, whether from Pessamit or Pointe-Bleue, we're all Innu. Thomas, you were born here, you got married here, you'll raise your children here. And if God so chooses, you will die here. The council has given its go-ahead. Here's the document."

He held a sheet of paper out to Thomas, who handed it to me. Thomas didn't know how to read, and I doubt the old chief could either. I never knew who had drafted the document. But I kept it. The paper is still in the wooden chest in my bedroom. It's yellowed and creased, but it's there.

The following week, a large truck unloaded a mountain of wood on the spot that had been granted to us, close to the shore and the lake. Two men from Roberval, recommended by Gros Bill, helped Thomas build the cabin. They showed up every morning and worked till nightfall. Little by little, the house took shape, an unusual structure in a village of tents.

The worksite drew many curious onlookers. Over time, we enlarged the cabin, but at first it was nothing but a small, square, one-storey building with one big room that served as entrance hall, kitchen and living room, and two bedrooms at the back. Light filtered through the chinks in the boards, and no one understood why we would want to overwinter there. Following Gros Bill's advice, Thomas insulated the walls with sawdust. He installed a wood stove.

Furniture was kept to a strict minimum: a table, straight-backed chairs, and an old oak beggar's bench donated to me by the priest—who was pleased to see a family settling in the village long-term—where we would store clothes.

There was neither electricity nor running water. Thomas set a big wooden barrel by the front door and attached a tin cup to it at the end of a string. This would be our water supply. In the bedrooms, we laid out two mattresses I had made of thick fabric stuffed with *mush* hair, which would make for warm, comfortable beds in the winter.

CHOICES

Once the house was built, we began preparing for our return to the territory. The closer the time came to leave, the bigger the knot in my stomach grew.

One evening late that summer, as we were getting some clothes ready, Christine offered to stay behind in Pointe-Bleue with Jeannette.

"You have your other children to look after, Manda."

"They could stay here too."

"Now listen here. You're not going to force them all to live on the reserve, are you? School's important, yes. But so is what they have to learn in the woods."

I stared at the floor, unable to look at my sister-in-law. "What about you, Christine? Won't that be hard on you?"

"Uh-uh," she said, dismissing my remark with a wave of her hand. "Someone has to be here for the little one, and it's better if it's me. Anyway, she's almost like a daughter to me too."

I was torn between the irresistible desire to leave and the feeling that it was my duty to stay behind since it had been my choice to send my daughter to school. I didn't know what to do. Christine settled the matter for me.

"Manda, your other children need you. You're not going to leave them without a mother at their age. Jeannette is older. The two of us will be fine here. Don't worry."

She was right. But by the same token, what right did I have to impose on my little ones an education that was foreign to them and, on top of that, to force this separation on my family? All my life, I have felt torn between what I saw as my duty and what my nature dictated.

I kissed Christine. She dried away the tears that trickled down my cheeks and hugged me tight.

Jeannette did not react well to the news that she would be staying behind while the rest of the family left for Passes-Dangereuses. She burst into tears, and I did my best to explain to her the importance of school. I didn't succeed.

For several years, Wabano, an Inuk nun, had been coming to Pointe-Bleue to teach French, catechism and mathematics. Despite my efforts to convey some of the same knowledge to my children over the winter, it wasn't enough.

"You can barely speak or write French. I can teach you some things in the woods, but you need a real teacher. You need to go to school."

"Maman! Papa speaks even less French than me."

Her red eyes pierced my heart.

"Next year, my child," Thomas said in his gentle

voice, "you'll return to the woods with us. You won't be alone. Your auntie Christine will stay with you, and you'll spend the winter in a fine house with heat and insulation. You won't have to put up with the cold of a tent. And don't worry about the forest, it's not going anywhere. It'll be there next year and the years after that. It's eternal."

How were we to know what was to come? Even though the signs were becoming obvious...sawmills multiplying, the railroad reaching Roberval, bringing ever more settlers and loggers, and Horace Beemer's huge steamships packed with tourists on Pekuakami. Maybe we felt we were safe. Maybe we preferred not to see the harbingers of progress that threatened us.

ABSENCES

It was the end of August and time for us to leave. We all attended mass. Jeannette cried silently, and I caressed her long black hair. Then our small caravan set out. I turned to look back. Barefoot in the sand, my daughter and Christine watched as we paddled away. My heart ached.

"When the river calls, Almanda, and its current is strong, we must follow," Thomas said.

He was right. Have faith in your heart. He taught me that too.

That winter turned out to be even harsher than the summer had been mild. It snowed almost every night, and we had to dig the camp out from under every morning. Thomas and Daniel spent almost all their time up north and came back only for Christmas. My chores kept my mind occupied, but I missed my husband, as well as Jeannette and Christine. As the weeks went by, the knot in my chest grew tighter. Fortunately, I could count on Malek's comforting presence.

That spring, we stopped off at Manouane Forks for just one day. The celebrations were short-lived for the Siméons. We resumed our journey, paddling at an accelerated pace. When Pointe-Bleue finally appeared on the horizon, I caught sight of our little house. On the porch, Christine sat waiting. The minute she spotted us, she waved vigorously, and Jeannette came at a run.

They helped us pull our canoes up onto shore. I hugged my daughter close, breathing in the perfume of her hair. She had grown, matured. Christine had taken good care of her.

Jeannette Siméon at the age of sixteen in front of Pekuakami

We unpacked. The next day, Thomas and I would sell our hides. But that evening, the whole family would eat together round the same fire. The knot in my stomach could unravel at last.

Other families followed our example afterward, leaving their children on the reserve for the winter so they could go to school. Little by little, the number of houses multiplied. Certain families held off because the children meant a helping hand during the hunt and they were loath to give that up. But every year, the number of pupils in the classroom grew. Nothing forced the parents to do so, but the Innu could see that the tide was turning and the world their descendants would face would be different from the one they had known.

Settlers kept arriving in greater and greater numbers, and new parishes sprang up. New loggers also arrived every day by train. But the forest was so huge no one worried. Nitassinan had enough wood for everyone, settlers as well as Innu. At least, that was what we thought.

PESSAMIT

Marie returned to us the following year after the death of her husband. She had five children. As for me, I had had nine, including Ernest. It made for a big family, and in the Siméon clan, everyone contributed to the young ones' education and wellbeing. There were many mouths to feed, but Anne-Marie, my eldest, was already a skilled trapper and hunter. We had missed her during the year she spent in Pointe-Bleue going to school.

In the Péribonka, we would occasionally happen upon other hunters who had come to try their luck, just as we did elsewhere. William Vallin, who was from Pessamit and whose parents had both died, often came as far as Passes-Dangereuses and Manouane Forks to hunt and trap with his partner, Dominic Saint-Onge. William was a cheerful, hard-working young man. He had a habit of firing a shot to announce his arrival as he approached the camp, a common practice among the Innu. He and Saint-Onge sometimes joined Thomas and Daniel on the great hunt. They shared the workload and the hides.

One day in March when we were at Manouane Forks, a shot rang out. Thomas went to see who it was. Anne-Marie, who was never far behind her father, recognized the visitors immediately.

"*Kuei*, William."

He smiled and waved. Thomas didn't fail to notice the batch of fine furs in the toboggans the two hunters pulled behind them.

"The hunt was good this winter."

"It would seem that luck smiled on us," William agreed. "It's the big guy who bagged most of them," he added with a laugh.

Dominic Saint-Onge, a giant of sorts with huge bear paws for hands and a face as round as a ball, always seemed to be smiling. He and William stayed on for a spell at the Forks. The days were getting longer, and the light of spring did everyone good after a hard winter.

Over the past year, Anne-Marie had spent a great deal of time with William. She was almost old enough to marry, and the prospect of seeing his eldest daughter leave the family nest worried her father.

"She's my eldest," he would say. "She does as much work as a man."

I understood his concern as a head of the clan. But I recognized in my daughter's eyes the light that had once shone in my own.

"Jeannette is growing up fast, Thomas. She's a good worker too. And the boys are here."

"The boys are still too young, Almanda. I would hate to see her go."

Thomas wasn't the kind of man to put obstacles in love's way, but Anne-Marie was almost indispensable to him in the woods.

"If someone had tried to come between you and me, do you think he would have succeeded?'

The two of us were alone in our tent by the stove. I was busy beading the shirt I'd made for Virginie, who was still tiny, and Thomas was finishing the carving of a cup-and-ball toy for Antonio. I took a sip of tea and snuggled close to him. He nodded. The question had been settled.

A week later, William asked for Anne-Marie's hand. He had waited for her sixteenth birthday. Thomas accepted, reluctantly. In July, Father Boyer, an oblate who had served in Pessamit on the North Shore, presided over the ceremony. That day took me back twenty years or so to the ceremony that had united me to Thomas, even though I was no longer anything like the young adventurer I had been then.

Shortly after, William and Anne-Marie left in a beautiful new canoe that Malek had made for them. They paddled as far as Chicoutimi. Although no Innu are left in that area today, at the time there were many. Then they followed Rivière Saguenay and the river the whites call Saint-Laurent to Pessamit. Along that great river, the Innu travel in large canoes where they hunt duck with harpoons. I saw them once when I went there with Thomas. You have to know how to read the sky if you venture out there because, if the wind takes you by surprise, you're lost.

At summer's end, it was with a heavy heart that

Thomas and I left for the Péribonka without our eldest daughter. It was not easy to say goodbye to the ones we loved in a world with neither telephone nor even mail, and we had to learn to live with their absence.

Anne-Marie Siméon

MISTOOK

Malek could neither count nor write, but no one would have dared to call him uneducated. He never spoke any language other than Innu-aimun. Yet he had a surname he had trouble pronouncing. When the missionaries converted the Indigenous peoples, they gave them their own names or those of other priests: Bacon, Fontaine, Mollen, or Jourdain. The Cree, our neighbours, who had lived with the English since the time of the first Hudson Bay posts, became Blacksmiths, Bossums, or Coons. The same occurred with every other nation.

Malek was the last of those who had known the world before the arrival of the white man, but he didn't talk about it. I never knew if he felt nostalgic for that bygone era. Most likely, the Innu tradition of sharing made the idea of the strangers' arrival easier to accept than it would have been for other peoples. For the whites, in any case. In the colony's beginnings, the Innu who, at the time, lived as far to the southwest as the Quebec City area, withdrew farther north and east to continue living as before. The territory was vast enough to provide for everyone. The concept of a territorial war did not exist for them.

The years held little sway over Malek, and death seemed to have passed him by. But that is never the case. Our time on earth is always short. When houses started going up in Pointe-Bleue, some of the elders chose to overwinter there. Malek never entertained that possibility.

"Stay with me, Papa," Christine said. "You'll help with the children."

"Next year, my daughter. Next year."

Malek even refused to sleep inside the house. He had only known life in the tent. It seemed to us that nothing would change as long as he was there, and in one sense, that was true. It was after his departure that our problems began.

That summer, his last, Malek often felt weak. In the morning, he'd come into the cabin, grab the cup hanging from the string nailed to the water barrel, fill it and take small sips. Then he'd sit on the bench without speaking. His profile, backlit by sunlight, seemed frailer by the day.

As usual, at the end of August he refused to stay behind. Yet this time, Thomas tried to persuade him. But his father, his bags at his side, waited for us on the morning of our departure. He took communion during mass, then slid into his canoe with the ease of an old hunter.

Pekuakami slept still to the murmur of our paddles. Malek had led the convoy to the Péribonka for many years. Today, he let his sons, Thomas and

Daniel, tackle the wind. How many kilometres had he himself covered thanks to the strength of his arms? In his mind, it was of no importance.

No rain, not much wind. A great deal of sunshine. Rivière Péribonka offered itself to this man who had loved it his entire life. Not hurrying, we reached Passes-Dangereuses within a month. We set up camp among large trees. The clan was ready to face the winter.

Malek only accompanied me occasionally on small hunts and he let me set the snares. He almost never left the camp now. Seated for long hours outside his tent, he looked off into the distance, likely to a place where game was plentiful. Anne-Marie made his meals, helped him get around. She had trouble hiding her sorrow at seeing him so diminished. Sometimes at night, after a good meal of hare, he'd regain his energy and sit with his grandchildren to tell them tales he'd learned from his father, north of Pessamit, a lifetime ago.

After Christmas, a wave of intense cold shrouded the region. The whole forest creaked. Game didn't dare to venture out. Once more, winter had us in its icy grip.

It worried Thomas to see the trouble his father had walking, and he decided to move the camp a bit farther south. We sat Malek in a toboggan that Thomas pulled after wrapping him in blankets and furs. We all had an extra load to tow, even the youngest. Mine included the tent, tools, and clothing. I wore a leather strap round my forehead to better distribute the weight and make my task easier. Despite the biting cold, we perspired advancing through the petrified forest.

Surrounded by his own people, the old nomad seemed serene. Years before, Malek had described for me what he imagined his last moments would be like.

"God created old age. Little by little, it deprives men of their strength, their sight, their hearing, of everything that makes living possible. This weakness obliges the others to help the old folk, to support them, to be generous. Old age benefits everyone. This was the Creator's will, Almanda."

His words came back to me as we slowly advanced, bathed in the northern sun's warmthless light. Malek had helped his father and his mother. His children did the same for him now. Life followed its course, forever a circle dictating the natural order.

That evening, Daniel and Thomas settled their father in the warmth of his tent. Anne-Marie slept next to him, ensuring the stove didn't run out of wood. Sometimes, we would stop for a couple of days to give him time to regain some strength. At that rate, it took us three weeks to reach Lac à la Carpe, north of Manouane Forks, where we pitched our tents in a thick pine grove. It was a perfect spot to brave the rest of the winter.

Malek seemed happy. He ate with us but asked to be put to bed fairly early. Anne-Marie spent long hours at her grandfather's side. The bond that united the two was strong. From the earliest days of his first granddaughter's life, he had been endlessly patient with her. Today, she looked after him, massaging his shoulders and arms when he complained of aches and pains, tending to the fire and entertaining him with stories. Sometimes, emerging from a deep slumber, his eyes would linger on Anne-Marie with an expression full of love.

For several weeks, it seemed like he was feeling better. His chest pains had disappeared, and he suffered less numbness. Thomas spent long stretches of time with his father. In silence, he held his hand.

The hunt continued to be a disappointment because of the intense cold. Mostly we survived on the few creatures we caught in our traps. But soon, we hoped, the wild geese would arrive.

Every morning, after doing the rounds of my snares, I headed for the river. With my axe, I'd dig a hole in the thick ice and throw in my lines. Sometimes I caught some fine walleye, which pleased Malek since it was his favourite fish.

"Ouananiche may be one of the mightiest," he said, "but walleye, with its firm flesh and buttery flavour, is the tastiest."

The days grew longer and, with the arrival of the first geese, the weather finally started to warm up. Anne-Marie and Jeannette brought a few back one afternoon, and I cooked them on the spit over the fire. The smell of grilled goose meat filled the tent and brought a glimmer of light to Malek's eyes. No doubt it was equally due to the pride the old hunter felt at his granddaughters' exploit. The feast announced that it was spring and that soon we would be returning to Pekuakami.

But Malek would never see the lake again. He died in his sleep that very night. The next morning the whole clan gathered round him one last time. I took my bible, and we prayed to the Creator, certain that, after such an exemplary life, Malek had rejoined Him. Anne-Marie and Jeannette shed all the tears they had inside. So did Thomas, Daniel, and Marie. The latter seemed to be, for the first time since I had met her, beside herself with grief. Like a wounded soul, she held her father's cold hand, her eyes brimming with tears, her throat constricted.

Our songs rose in one voice, that of Malek's family, between the trees and the mountains, pushed by the east wind up to the sky. At least that was our hope.

The snow was still too deep for us to bury him, and in any case, the ground itself was as hard as rock. After praying all day, we packed our bags and broke camp the next day at dawn. Thomas and Daniel laid their father's body on a toboggan, wrapped in a shroud of beautiful caribou hides. The whole family headed south.

As we advanced, the weather grew warmer and the granular snow could no longer bear the weight of our snowshoes, which kept sinking. But no one complained. Exhausted from days of tough trekking through the forest, we finally reached Mistook. At the time, it was only a hamlet not far from Alma with a few houses clustered round a pretty church made of wooden planks topped by a silver steeple. The rutted earthen road was almost impassable for carts.

We pitched our tents by the cemetery. The next

morning, the priest held a funeral in the deserted church. Our songs accompanied Malek Siméon to his final resting place. Searching through the small graveyard, you can still find his tombstone today.

The next day, Thomas, Daniel, and his partner returned to the Péribonka, and Marie and I stayed behind with the children. By the time the men returned, the snow had melted and their canoes were overflowing with hides. My eldest daughter's round belly announced she would be giving birth that summer in Pointe-Bleue. Thomas was now the head of the family, and we were about to become grandparents. Life is a circle. As I was reminded by fate once again.

NAUSEA

There had been harbingers for some time already.
Farmers had cleared land and encircled the lake.
The smell of manure hung in the air. New villages
sprang into existence and several church steeples
rose now in the skies of Nitassinan. Loggers in particular were increasingly numerous and active. They
had begun with the trees round the lake and the
villages. Then they'd gone farther back into the
woods. We crossed paths with them from time to
time at Baie de la Pipe. Sometimes we would come
across an area they'd run rampant over. The loggers
left nothing behind but swamps beset by clouds of
blackflies.

Whenever we stumbled onto a clearcut, Thomas,
usually so calm, would fly into a rage.

"It's not enough for them to chop down trees," he
fumed, "they fell every life form—birds, animals—
they slaughter the spirit of the forest itself. How can
men be so cruel?"

Thomas was right. But his reasoning was that
of an Innu man who knows he will always return

to retrace his steps. A logger, however, keeps on marching straight ahead, never looking back. He tracks progress.

In the years following Malek's death, we began to see more and more trails bringing men and their machines ever deeper into the woods. Maybe our elder would have known how to prepare us. Just when we needed it the most, we could no longer count on his wisdom to guide us.

Nitassinan was changing, but we refused to see it. Or maybe we simply could not? How could we imagine a forest razed? Time sped up, but we continued to live to the rhythm of a dying forest, since we knew no other.

That summer was mild and rainy. When it drew to a close, excited, we prepared our bags as usual. Before the departure, the Innu filed into Pointe-Bleue's church, and our songs rose into the warm air. After taking communion, the whole clan put their canoes into the water. Pekuakami barely stirred. It was as though it knew and was holding its breath.

After three days, as we approached the mouth of Rivière Péribonka, the air reeked with the nausea-inducing smell of damp wood. On the lake floated a huge, dark, rippling mass. Not one of us had ever seen anything like it. It was only as we drew near that we understood.

Thousands of felled trees bobbed on the surface of Pekuakami, borne by the current. The wood came from the river. Our river, on which men danced, armed with long lances whose tips were fitted with metal hooks with which they freed any logs pushed between the rocks by the current.

We sat paralyzed with fear in our canoes. Before us Rivière Péribonka, suffocating under the weight of all those logs, vomited the forest into the lake.

THE LOG DRIVERS

Log drivers had taken over Rivière Péribonka. A group of individuals stood talking round a pile-up caused by an eddy. Hundreds of overlapping logs formed a jam that blocked the drive. The men were losing patience. Something had to be done, but they didn't seem to agree on what that should be.

One of them, who looked to be the oldest and wore a wide-brimmed hat, tied sticks of dynamite to the end of a pole, which he plunged under the tangle of logs. He lit a long wick, and everyone ran back over the floating logs toward shore to take cover. The explosion projected clouds of scum into the air. Around our boats, dead fish surfaced, their bellies white in the filthy water.

Tears ran down my cheeks and rage filled my heart. We drew ashore and Thomas headed toward the man with the hat—a tall, cold fellow whose features were as sharp as the blade of a knife.

"Speak French, Indian, I don't understand a word you're saying."

Thomas tried, but the other man would have none of it. I cut in.

"Do you understand me?"

He stared, undoubtedly surprised to hear me address him in his language without the lilting Innu accent.

"What do you want? You can't stay here, it's dangerous. Clear out."

"What did you do to the river?"

The head driver stared at me, incredulous.

"This is the log drive, my little lady. The Price company has opened a lumber camp up there," he said, pointing his pipe upriver, "and we bring the logs down."

"How are we supposed to get round it to travel up north?"

With hindsight, I realize how naïve my reaction was. The man laughed. Then, puffing on his pipe, he finally seemed to understand who we were. And, above all, where we were going.

"No one gets by."

I drew nearer and stared him down. He fidgeted with his hat to try to regain his composure.

"The drive starts at Lac Péribonka. Loggers are busy felling trees at Manouane too, and I've got men on that river as well. You can't roam here, the land belongs to the company. Go home."

The head driver turned to his men, directing them to free a pile of logs.

"I haven't finished speaking to you."

He no longer seemed to hear me.

"There's no way we're going to *go home*, as you put it."

I raised my voice, and the head driver shouted orders at his men.

I pushed the man, and he just about fell. At last, he turned round and glared at me, raising his fist. He had barely stirred before Thomas grabbed him by the throat, with Daniel right beside him holding his Winchester at the ready.

The man spread his arms wide.

"Hey, I'm not the one who decides. I'm just the head driver. My job is to make sure the logs are transported under the best possible conditions. The plot of land along Rivière Péribonka belongs to Frank Ross."

"The forest doesn't belong to Ross."

"Madame, he paid the government for it. He's within his rights. Go home."

"Our home is up there!"

Now I was the one shouting.

"My children were born in the Péribonka, that's where we live."

I felt like weeping tears of rage, and the head driver must have noticed. He adopted a gentler tone and drew closer.

"Go back to Pointe-Bleue, Madame. In any event, canoes can no longer get through here. I'm sorry."

He got back to business, running deftly over the logs, barking orders. We watched the river, or what the river had become. The stench of waterlogged wood filled our nostrils. Before us, dozens of men busied themselves. Farther north, loggers were chopping down our forest while the men here were tasked with transporting it to the pulpmill. Who had the power to do all that without even asking our opinion?

None of us dared leave; we sat motionless in our boats for the longest time. It was Marie who finally took Thomas by the arm. We couldn't stay here, she said. It was best that we return to Pointe-Bleue.

Almost all of our rivers were subjected to the drive, and over the next few days, just like us, several families returned to Pointe-Bleue. Methodically, the logging companies went about building roads to go ever deeper into the forest to cut even more timber.

We stayed put on the reserve. In fact, there was nowhere else to go. The wood fed the pulp and paper mills and the sawmills. The mills gave work to the settlers. Progress had finally arrived. That's what people believed. But life is a circle. Time would be sure to remind them of that one day.

I didn't see the Péribonka again for years. When I finally did travel to the region decades later in a pickup truck with Antonio, I didn't recognize it. The road passes behind Saint-Ludger-de-Milot and crosses the mountains. There are all kinds of cottages and almost no trees left. We pitched our tents on the shore of a lake.

A ranger, a young man in his twenties, approached us.

"You all have bagged some game. Have you got a permit?"

"We're Indian, we have a right to hunt here."

He looked at me, and I saw scorn deep in his eyes. Tall and sturdy, he had a ruddy complexion, and to him, with my plaid skirt, the cross round my neck, my beret and my pipe, I was just an old Indian. A savage.

"You don't have the right."

He tried to grab my rifle, and Antonio jumped him. The two rolled around on the ground. When my son stood up, the other man, a foot taller than he was, lay there knocked senseless, his eye swollen, blood in his mouth.

"Come on, Antonio, we're leaving. He'll be sure to make trouble for us."

I never saw that man again, and I never returned to the Péribonka. But I think about it every day.

Floating log booms on Lac Kénogami

BOOMTOWN

Cut off from our territory, we had to learn to live differently. To switch from a life on the move to a sedentary existence. We didn't know how to go about it and still don't today. Boredom set in and distilled its bitterness through our souls.

Those who had houses shut themselves up inside; the others pitched their tents by the lake. The first winter in Pointe-Bleue was horrific. The wind flew across the frozen surface and swept through the village of cabins and tents. The government had handed out subsidies to the families to help them get by. Otherwise, we would have starved to death since there was not enough game around the reserve for everyone. The Innu went from autonomy to dependency. We are still grappling with the consequences.

There was little to do in Pointe-Bleue. Our knowledge was worth nothing there. Men like Thomas felt empty, and the light in their eyes was gradually extinguished. There was no need to kill us. All they had to do was starve us and watch us slowly die.

Many sought refuge in alcohol. Can you blame them for wanting to numb the pain? Some tried to farm the surrounding fields. They made for strange farmers. Some worked as guides for outfitters. Like Thomas, Daniel, and my sons on a luxurious property in Parc des Laurentides. Helping rich strangers bring hunting trophies back to Chicago, New York, or somewhere in Michigan was humiliating work, but at least they were out in the woods.

Others got hired onto lumber camps, where they were given small, poorly paid jobs that boiled down to helping the very loggers who had dispossessed them. Those men came back broken.

Roberval experienced a boom. The lumber camps attracted new inhabitants. Houses and streets had to be built to make room for them all. New stores opened their doors, a brick plant, a foundry, a wool mill, even a canoe manufacturer. The poor farmers' village was transformed into an industrious and prosperous town.

Gros Bill, who was raking in money with his sawmill, didn't lack for lumber to be transformed into planks.

"Companies fight over the forest round Lac Saint-Jean," he explained to me one day when I dropped by to purchase boards for an addition to our cabin. "Price, Quebec Development, Chicoutimi's Pulp Company, all of them stuff politicians' pockets full with their bribes. The lumber goes to the highest bidder, Madame Siméon. That's the way it is."

"That's what you call progress?"

William Girard just shrugged.

My sisters-in-law and I spent our time making prettily patterned birchbark baskets, *mush*-hide moccassins, beaded mittens, jewellery and all the objects that used to be part of our everyday life. We sold them in a craft store. My youngest son, Gérard, gave us a hand. In no time, the snowshoes he made became extremely popular. He even received orders from rich Americans looking for authentic birchbark canoes, for which they were prepared to pay a small fortune.

I always hated the word "crafts." But they allowed us to keep the knowledge within the family. It was our last treasure.

RAILWAY

I hate trains. I hate the railroad tracks that tear up the countryside, the locomotives that stink and shriek.

When the railway arrived in Roberval, it was nothing but a modest parish of farmers, a village with a few buildings clustered round a church. Indians and whites lived peaceably on the shore of Pekuakami. The train changed all that.

Carriages from the Quebec and Lake St-John Railway linked Roberval to the rest of the world thanks to a long path logged through the forest to Quebec City. From there, the tracks headed east, west, and south. The farmers, who had lived more or less in a state of self-sufficiency up to that point, could now, thanks to the refrigerated compartments, ship their crops, butter, milk, and cream to the big cities to the south. And those train cars returned with more settlers and loggers in their bellies.

And the railway brought to our home a race we had never seen before: tourists.

The trains allowed Horace Beemer, a voraciously ambitious American businessman, to make his fortune. He built Roberval's railway, then had a saw-mill built. And finally, a luxury hotel the likes of which no one had ever seen before on the shores of Pekuakami, a veritable chateau — which is what people did, in fact, call it — that could accommodate hundreds of guests.

In Roberval, everyone thought he was crazy. But tourists came by the trainload, mostly from the United States, drawn by the beauty of Nitassinan and the majestic Pekuakami.

To keep them entertained, Beemer organized all kinds of activities. He built playgrounds and croquet lawns. He even had bears trapped and kept them in cages, greatly impressing his customers. As though *mashk* was a plaything. Several years later, when a raging fire razed Château Roberval, it is said that Horace Beemer died of sorrow and exhaustion. I have always thought it was the spirit of the *mashk* repaying him in kind.

Most people came to take advantage of the waters teeming with fish. They crisscrossed Pekuakami on steamboats, like the ones on the Mississippi River in Mark Twain's novels. They fished in the lake and its rivers hoping to catch ouananiche. Business was so good that Beemer had a second hotel built across the lake on an island not far from Rivière Péribonka. Steamboats connected the chateau and the Island House, which looked like a large fishing lodge.

Money flowed freely. Thanks to the railway, the long-hoped-for prosperity had finally come to pass, and every town wanted its own train station.

Chicoutimi got its station five years later, Laterrière the following year, then it was Saint-Félicien's turn. To reach them, the railway had to go through Pointe-Bleue. Of course, no one asked us what we thought, and the engineers never considered bypassing our community.

At noon one day, two employees of the Quebec and Lake St-John Railway knocked on my door.

"The train will be coming right through here, Madame," said the one who looked to be the boss as he pointed at the bushes in front of my home. "We're going to have to demolish your house."

The man threatening to raze the cabin I had gone to such great lengths to have built was a rather tall, dry fellow with stooped shoulders and glasses that perched on his thin nose. His delicate black mous-tache gave him the look of a country doctor. He wore a wool suit, and a gold watch chain hung from his vest.

"You want to demolish my house?"

"You will, of course, be compensated, Madame."

I stepped out onto the porch, shut the door behind me, and stared at the railway company employee.

"No."

He looked disconcerted.

"What do you mean, no? It wasn't a question. The route has already been decided."

I crossed my arms. He gave me a funny look. I imagine those fellows weren't used to being told no. I turned my back on him and returned inside.

The next day, the train company men knocked on

my door again. The employee of the Quebec and Lake St-John Railway, his hand in his vest pocket, kept tapping his watch.

"Good day, Madame."

I eyed him scornfully, and he held my gaze.

"You misunderstood me yesterday, Madame. I didn't come here to ask for your permission. The train is going to pass through here," he said, pointing with his long arm at the route he wanted to build at a stone's throw from my house. "We can't bypass your house because of the embankment back there. The company has obtained all the necessary authorizations. You'll be compensated."

"I don't give a damn about your papers. This is our home, you're on a reserve, you won't force me to leave."

"Listen, Madame. I understand this can't be very pleasant. But we'll build you another house, a brand-new one, just a bit farther back. Better than what you have, if I may say so."

He had pulled his watch out of his pocket and was sliding it through his fingers, the gold sparkling in the sun.

"No."

"You can't say no. This is the procedure."

He had raised his voice, and he glared at me the way men do who think they have every right.

"This isn't a tent. If you're not happy, build around it."

I spun on my heel and shut the door. He stayed put on the porch, his pocket watch in his sweaty hand.

A few weeks later, the railroad neared Pointe-Bleue. Workers swarmed round it morning to night, cutting wood and pounding tracks into the ground with a sledgehammer. The railway to Saint-Félicien was finished in 1917. It passed a few metres from my front door. The engineers didn't divert the track.

When the train entered Pointe-Bleue for the first time, we initially thought it was an earthquake. The cabin started shaking like a leaf in the wind. The windows banged, the walls seemed about to collapse. A dull roar sounded, and dishes toppled over in the cupboards. The children started to cry. Everyone rushed outside, fear in their belly, and the train hurtled by with a shriek. When at last it had disappeared and the house had quit shaking, we stood there across from the empty tracks.

My son Antonio shot me a frightened glance.

"Maman, what was that?"

"What?"

"The train!"

"What train, Antonio?"

"That one, Maman," he replied, pointing at the convoy as it disappeared. "It just about knocked our house over."

"There is no train here, my son. Let's go back inside."

The train was inflicted on me, and for years I ignored it. I still ignore it. The tracks still run past my door, but there are almost no trains anymore. Apparently, Canadian National Railway is thinking of abandoning passenger trains out this way.

It doesn't make much difference to me. That train never existed. And our house is still where Thomas built it with his own two hands. It will always be here.

THE BREAKING POINT

The years passed, leaving me with memories of grey. By forcing us to stay in Pointe-Bleue, they wanted to turn us into people like them. Dispossessed nomads, we could only be what we were, people without a country.

After our land, they took the one thing left to us: our children.

One morning, four seaplanes appeared on the horizon. They circled Pointe-Bleue, tilting their wings in the sky. Then they nose-dived and landed on Pekuakami, just across from our house. The pilots guided their dancing craft to shore while RCMP officers arrived by truck via the road from Roberval. Federal officials preceded them in a large sedan as black as a crow, which they parked across from the planes.

A Mountie got out of the car and ordered everyone to gather round.

"My name is Sergeant Leroux. We are here to take the children to residential school. Canada will give them a respectable education."

People surrounded the officer and Father Jodoin,

the parish priest who accompanied him. The sergeant had a stentorian tone, and his words echoed like thunder.

"All children between the ages of six and fifteen will attend school. Gather up your belongings, the planes will be leaving in an hour's time."

The Mounties fanned out through the village, going from house to house. Some parents refused to let them take their young ones. The discussion became heated at times. The officers' weapons were plainly visible. At one point, an official raised his voice. He was a rather puny-looking man wearing a brown suit that was too tight. He wore metal-rimmed glasses, and his voice crackled with a frostiness that made the blood run cold.

"You have no money to educate and feed them properly. Look at your children! They don't know how to read or write. They're skinny. They look like real savages. In school, they'll be adequately fed and housed. They'll learn to read and write. Church men and women will be in charge of their education. It's better for them this way."

"You have no right to take our children," Antonio said to the Mountie.

"If you refuse, the army will take them away," the government official retorted. "Don't try to play games with the government. You have no choice. Indians have to learn to read like other Canadians. It's as simple as that. The hour has come, even for savages, to get with the times."

In a cold voice, the official explained that the

children would spend the academic year in residential school. That they would be well treated there and that it was an opportunity for their parents to see their offspring receive a good education. But many parents protested. The Mounties started to get jittery and they kept their hands on their guns.

The man wearing a cassock, who had said nothing so far, spoke up. He stressed the fact that the Church would take care of the children.

"I hope you don't intend to go against the will of God and the good Sainte Anne," he said in his suave voice.

Sainte Anne is our patron saint. Even I was shaken by his words.

The Mounties took the children by canoe out to the planes. Some of them, not knowing how to swim, cried, afraid of falling into the water. The boats returned to shore empty, and the aircraft began drifting away. Their engines roared, and the metal birds made their way farther out onto the lake. Their bellies heavy, they rose into the sky, then veered west carrying my grandchildren and the others. Onshore, a sense of shame spread among all those who had not found the strength to oppose the will of Ottawa and Rome. The planes disappeared, swallowed up by clouds.

We knew nothing about Fort George, their destination. The priest had told us it was an island located in Cree territory on the boundary of Inuit lands, at the far end of La Grande Rivière. The Innu knew of the river that throws itself into the northern sea, but none of us had ever been to that place, hundreds of kilometres away from Pointe-Bleue.

The next day, an ominous calm reigned. Try to imagine a village emptied of its children.

The months unfurled slowly on the shore of Pekuakami. That winter was even gloomier and sadder than the ones that had preceded it. We had no news of the little ones. Despite the priest's intervention, many parents blamed themselves for having let their young ones go. But it was too late for regrets. Thomas continued to hunt round Pointe-Bleue, even though game was increasingly scarce. All the land had been cleared, and great distances had to be covered to reach the forest. As for me, in order to forget, I threw myself into my handiwork.

In June, the planes returned and the whole village ran to the shore. The children's hair had been cut, they wore the same clothing as the whites, and something had vanished from their eyes. Or perhaps from ours.

I was there with the others on the strand, searching among all the tired faces for my family. When I saw Antonio's eldest daughter, Jeannette, named after his favourite sister, walking toward us alone, I felt a stab of anguish. Where was Julienne?

"Where's your little sister, Jeannette?"

"I don't know."

Her voice trembled. Antonio looked at me, worried. The priest who'd brought the little ones home came over to us.

"The child fell ill this winter. Her condition worsened, and she had to be rushed to hospital in

Montréal. Unfortunately, the doctors weren't able to save her. We said many a prayer for her."

Antonio's wife threw herself onto her knees, uttering a cry that rent the sky. My son stared at the priest, incredulous. No one had thought to tell the family.

"She had something wrong with her heart," he continued.

"My granddaughter never had problems with her health," I cut in.

"I'm not a doctor, Madame Siméon. She started to feel unwell. We had no choice but to send her to hospital since all we have in Fort George is a small clinic."

My daughter-in-law was shaking like a leaf. I hugged her tightly. Antonio enfolded Jeannette in his arms, and we stood on the shore weeping together.

That night in bed, I clung to Thomas. For once, the contact of his skin against mine wasn't enough to chase away the ache in my belly or to bring warmth to our bed.

We never did learn what happened, or what our little girl suffered from, other than the mention of her heart. Had she even been ill? No one in the family had ever suffered from a similar illness.

Later on, when all the horror stories about residential schools began circulating, I wondered what really happened to Julienne but never received an answer.

Julienne Siméon between her cousins Catherine Basile and
Marthe Vollant at the Fort George residential school

THE DAMAGE DONE

My children were born in the woods. My grand-children grew up on a reserve. The former were educated on the land, the latter in a residential school. When they returned, they spoke French. The white priests forbade them from speaking Innu-aimun and even punished those who did. Another tie had been severed between the generations. They thought that by robbing our children of their language they would make them white. But an Innu who speaks French is still Innu. With yet another wound.

For the first time in our history, Innu youth no longer turned to their elders for their teachings. Worse still, they were suspicious of them because their teachers had drummed in the lesson that their illiterate parents were savages, uneducated, backward. From hearing it so often, they ended up believing it.

When, at summer's end, the planes reappeared, the children returned to Fort George. Another winter without them awaited us. That too fed our anger.

Thomas managed to kill enough moose to supply

us with hides. Our beaded mocasins and mittens sold
well, as did our birchbark baskets. We worked long
hours, and Gérard, my youngest, continued to help
us. Clément accompanied his father in the woods.
Antonio often stayed behind to drink. Some sorrows
leave indelible scars on the heart.

Clément Siméon paddling up Rivière Péribonka

We began noticing phenomena that we had never
experienced before in Pointe-Bleue. Men spent all
day drinking, then beat their wives. Mothers drank
too, even when pregnant, and fought amongst themselves. In the past, people would drink come summer,
but never the rest of the year, because no one brought
liquor out onto the land. Now that everyone stayed in
Pointe-Bleue, many had nothing better to do.

There were also a number of train accidents. People who were intoxicated would walk along the tracks, oblivious to the locomotives. Some fell asleep there, night or day. After several tragic deaths, the train started slowing down the minute it entered the Pointe-Bleue area, and the conductor sounded the whistle the whole time he was on the reserve. They still do that today.

The first suicides were a shock. We had never seen one before. What brought people to the brink of such despair? Their numbers kept growing. Suddenly, there was an epidemic of deaths.

Yet, from the outside, the situation on the reserve seemed to have improved. We were building new houses, stores were opening their doors. The old tent village began to look more like a modern community. Progress, finally. But the signs of distress piled up: dilapidated homes, dirt roads where the young roamed late on summer nights.

Alcohol and violence were not the problem. They were the symptoms of the insidious sickness eating away at the Innu.

THE BLOCK OF FOURTEEN APARTMENTS

My daughter Jeannette fell in love with one of the workers building the railroad. The illegitimate son of an Indian man, he had white status and, in marrying him, my daughter was stripped of her Indian status. Just another way of making us disappear. She was forced to leave the reserve. But in the city where she and her children were the only ones with brown skin, everyone knew what they were. Jeannette raised ten children, nine of them girls, in the city. At least, by growing up where whites lived, they were able to avoid residential school.

Alma was a town made up of houses perched on the sloping banks of the stream known as La Petite Décharge. The water stank of pulp from the paper-mill, where François-Xavier, Jeannette's husband, worked. He made a good salary that allowed him to feed his family. Jeannette dreamed of moving out of their apartment block.

I went to visit her once. We left in Clément's old truck on a pilgrimage to Sainte-Anne-de-Beaupré and stopped off in Alma. Our group included Marie and Christine, as well as my daughters Anne-Marie and Virginie with their husbands. We pitched our tents for the night behind the apartment block where Jeannette lived. Its massive four-storey silhouette loomed over the other more modest buildings in town. Spiral staircases gave access to wide balconies out front and back. Fourteen families were crowded inside.

As for the anglos, they lived higher up on the other side of Rivière La Grande Décharge in Riverbend, a well-to-do district with rows of small, elegant houses beneath trees.

Word of our presence swept through the town like wildfire. Neighbours poked their heads out their windows. Others who lived farther away came by car. The whole town wanted to see the savages. Onlookers commented on the strangeness of our clothing, our long hair, our tents. They took our reserved manner for wildness. Their distrust alarmed us. The colour of our skin contrasted too strongly with the white of that town.

We left the next morning at dawn. The worst thing was not the wary looks; I couldn't care less about that. But Jeannette's children's self-consciousness over the embarrassment caused by their family was heartbreaking. What hurt the most was that I understood it. After we left, the children would be subjected to jeers and teasing. Even in town, it wasn't easy to be Innu.

SIDEWALKS

A mere six kilometres from our home, Roberval continued to grow. The first time I set foot there, with my aunt and uncle, it was still nothing but a large village with a few stores clumped together along the dirt road that bordered Pekuakami.

Prosperity turned it into a town with fine paved avenues and stores fitted out with attractive window displays. There were restaurants, a movie theatre, firefighters, police, a brass band that paraded every summer on Saint-Jean-Baptiste Day. Several schools and two churches had been built. And bars kept their doors open till late at night. Workers from the mills and logging camps spent their wages there.

Drawn by the beauty of the Innu women, several of them drove out to Pointe-Bleue bearing bottles of liquor. With nothing to do and flattered by all the attention, some of the girls let themselves be seduced. In Innu culture, women rendezvous with men before marriage. It helps them make the right choice of partner. Since life in the woods can be demanding, the two have to be able to get along.

It wasn't rare to see a car roaring erratically through the people walking down our streets devoid of sidewalks, the echo of the occupants' crude laughter and cries following in their wake.

One June morning, a mother and father found their eight-year-old boy lying in a ditch, his body broken, his face covered in clotted blood. They saw no sign of brakes having been applied. The tragic death of a child sowed consternation throughout the community.

The following Saturday, the church was overflowing. In his homily, the priest spoke of the fragility of life and of the need to place one's faith in the Creator. We prayed to Sainte Anne.

Two weeks later, one evening after dark, a car killed a twelve-year-old girl while she was crossing the street. The driver said she appeared suddenly and he couldn't stop his sports car in time. The child's head hit the windshield and the impact threw her body into the mud. Witnesses claimed the car was going at an excessive speed, but the man at the wheel, the sawmill manager, denied it. Once again, four days later, we all crowded together inside the church, our hearts heavy.

Not long after, a reckless driver caused the death of yet another young victim. A bottle of whisky was found on the back seat of the car. But the driver argued that the child had come out of nowhere and it would have been impossible to avoid hitting him. People encircled the driver. Anger brewed. The sirens of the police car and the ambulance rang out. Nothing more could be done for the child, and the Mountie managed to calm the crowd down. I was there on the street. The accident happened not far from my house, as I was coming home from the beach, where I liked to spend the evening by a campfire.

The driver stank of alcohol. In Roberval, when a policeman stops a drunk driver, he makes him walk a straight line to see how drunk he is. In Pointe-Bleue, there are no paved roads on which to draw any lines.

I went to the band council and demanded that they intercede with the government. The councillors and the chief agreed, but who would listen to them? I lost my temper and was told to calm down. In view of all the innocent victims, nothing could appease my anger.

The following summer, reckless drivers killed six more youngsters. Every time, it was the same scenario. A certain apathy took hold among the inhabitants of Pointe-Bleue. What could we do?

While Thomas was away working for the outfitter, I asked Clément to drive me to the Canadian National Railway train station, the CNR having replaced the Quebec and Lake St-John Railway. Roberval had changed considerably over the years. I discovered that the former parish was now a city. The streets, wide and clean, were paved and had sidewalks lined with all kinds of stores whose colourful signs vied for customers' attention.

That day, the wind blew from the north and whipped up Pekuakami's waters. But the din of the city, a combination of roaring engines and the chatter of passersby, masked the roar of the lake's waves.

The most impressive building in terms of size was the hospital located at the end of a row of houses, between the fields and the boundless blue. Across from the monastery, the Ursulines had established a huge sanatorium whose brick facade was almost two hundred metres long. The building had two wings of equal size set at an angle to each other.

Outfitted with stone apertures, stacked balconies and many windows and stained glass, the five-storey building could, it was said, house more than four hundred patients, most of whom suffered from tuberculosis. The nuns had chosen Roberval for the purity of Pekuakami's air, and the site took in victims of the great TB epidemic from across the region.

The old train station had undergone quite a transformation. The original building with its arrow-shaped dormer windows had almost tripled in size since 1888. It was now a long edifice with a slanted roof. Employees bustled all around. A cart waited out front, two bicycles were propped up against the wooden wall. Inside, an employee stood behind a wicket fitted with iron bars. He looked up. Instinctively, to keep my composure, I stroked the large cross hanging round my neck.

"I'd like a ticket for Quebec City."

The man was thirty or so, with a round face and a bald scalp. He wore a white, high-collared shirt and a black vest. His equally black tie throttled his neck.

He stared at me with pinched lips. Did I really look that strange with my long grey hair coiled on either side of my head beneath my beret?

"A ticket for Quebec City," I said again.

The CNR employee blinked and gave a little cough as though to clear his throat. He held out a small piece of paper.

"The train from Saint-Félicien will be here in two hours."

I took the ticket and stepped outside. I sat on a bench facing the tracks, struck a match on my skirt and drew on my pipe. I had set out on a whim, propelled by anger and the need to shake up the passivity that had taken hold in the community. Pointe-Bleue lived in the hope that something would happen. But life trickled on like sand through an hourglass while all around us the world continued to accelerate.

The train's arrival woke me from slumber. The tracks squealed under the weight of the steel monster. The locomotive spat out clouds of soot that sullied the sky. I gathered up my bag and jumped on board. The compartment was nearly deserted. I sat by the window. The train started up almost immediately. Its steam turbines shrieked. Soon we were racing between the lake and the fields. In the distance was the tree line.

The itinerary called for a stop in every village. Slowly, the compartment filled with travellers. Past Desbiens, the tracks veered to the right and headed south. Ahead, the mountains stood out against the sky.

With my cheek glued to the window, I watched familiar landscapes fly by. The railroad followed former Innu trails. Vast portions of the forest had been logged, and the sight of the territory transformed into an arid swamp broke my heart. Where had all the animals gone? Had they too been put on reserves?

Exhausted and distraught, I fell asleep. It was dark out when I was woken by the squeal of brakes. We advanced, slowly now, through suburbs that must have housed hundreds of people. To the left, I could make out the lights of Quebec City's harbour and, ahead, the train station.

I had never seen anything like it. With its cylindrical towers topped by the point of a tarnished copper roof, the building looked like the medieval castles described in the books I used to read to my children in the tent. In the distance loomed a rock headland on top of which the city's lights danced. The train entered the imposing facility, and we found ourselves in a huge covered tunnel, where it came to a halt.

"End of the line. Everyone off!" cried an employee, who wore a cap and a double-breasted uniform trimmed with gold buttons.

The passengers leapt to their feet and began gathering their belongings. I waited for the compartments to empty, then picked up my bag and stepped outside.

The station hall was an enormous room whose tiled and vaulted ceiling looked as though it had been lowered onto its tall brick walls. Beautiful mosaics decorated the marble floor. I sank onto a wooden bench. I ate a bit of dried meat and waited for day to break.

THE CHIEF

It was the light pouring through the glass roof that woke me. The hall was bathed in the brilliance of morning. I set out.

The station faced an imposing rock promontory. I started up a steep slope that led past a hospital almost as big as the one in Roberval and from there to a bustling street.

Delivery trucks unloaded their merchandise destined for various stores. I stepped into a small restaurant. The interior made me think of a cave dug into the rock. I sat next to the window. The server, an energetic woman of fifty or so, took a long look at me, probably wondering what this old Indian was doing there. I ordered toast and some tea, which I sipped slowly. Closing my eyes, I could almost imagine myself back at home. Tea has always had a calming effect on me.

I asked directions of the server, who showed me which road to take. Following her directions, I walked west between rows of pretty stone houses. Once I passed the fortifications, the Quebec parliament loomed to my left, a huge building set in a large public square. At the entrance was a sculpture of an Indian wearing a strange get-up unlike anything I'd ever seen before.

Inside, an employee assisted me, and I soon found what I was looking for. The door was open, and I made my way over to a woman seated behind a desk. Wearing a pink suit, she had stark features and short hair. Her thin lips and glasses made her look like a schoolteacher. I stood there for a good while before she deigned to look up in order to shoot a steely glance.

"What can I do for you?" she asked in a curt voice.

"I've come to see Maurice Duplessis."

She frowned, then eyed me up and down.

"I don't see an appointment in the premier's schedule," she said, pretending to consult a large notebook.

"I have to speak to him. It's important."

"I'm sorry, Madame. Monsieur Duplessis is a very busy man..."

I interrupted her.

"Listen here, Madame, I have come from Pointe-Bleue to speak to him. I am not budging till I've seen him."

"In any event, Monsieur Duplessis is away."

"I'll wait for him."

I sat in one of the chairs at the far end of the waiting area, my bag on my lap.

"As you wish, but I'm warning you, you're wasting your time."

She stressed the last word. I pursed my lips. I took out one of the novels I'd brought with me and dove in.

Not much happens in the hushed atmosphere of a premier's office graced only by smartly dressed people. The secretary answers the telephone from time to time. She works at the typewriter, preparing letters that the mailboy picks up.

I was used to waiting. Patience is a virtue for a hunter. But at five o'clock, the woman gathered her belongings, got to her feet and came over to me.

"We're closing. I told you, Monsieur Duplessis is away."

I got up, grabbed my bag and walked out. I felt weary. I walked along the fortification to the south and sat down on the grass in a secluded spot. I spread out a woollen blanket. I had food with me: dried meat, blueberries, and bannock. Then I lay down on the grass. I was used to sleeping under the stars.

The next morning, I returned to the parliament building at nine o'clock. Maurice Duplessis's secretary didn't greet me when I sat in the same chair at the far end of the room. I dove into my book. Men carrying briefcases came and went. None looked like Duplessis. How long would I have to wait? There was no way I would return home without speaking to him. Even though, ever since the Indian Act, we were under the federal government's jurisdiction, I was certain that a person such as Maurice Duplessis could help us.

At home, no one had tried to convince me to abandon my plan. Everyone knew there was no point.

At the same time as the day before, the secretary got to her feet and gathered up her belongings. I strolled through the city for a while, walking down sidewalks amid a large crowd. Certain restaurants had tables set up out front and people dined outside, which seemed like quite a lovely idea to me. I walked as far as Château Frontenac, a building even more imposing than the old train station, one that reminded me of Horace Beemer's former hotel in Roberval. From the huge terrace overlooking the river, I could see Nitassinan's mountains in the distance.

Once again, I returned to spend the night by the fortified wall. Watching the stars above, my heart heavy, I thought of Thomas, off in the woods, unaware of my presence here.

On the third day, the secretary looked at me with a hint of exasperation. Nonetheless, she motioned for me to approach.

"Monsieur Duplessis is back. But do not kid yourself. His schedule is still very full. He has meetings all day long."

"I'm not leaving till I speak to him. Tell him that, please."

She shrugged. I returned to my spot at the back of the room.

An hour later, a man hurried inside. He was of medium height with slightly bowed shoulders, and his profile was that of an eagle. He grabbed the document the woman held out to him and swept into the office. Was that him? How could I be sure? The most I had seen of Maurice Duplessis was his picture in the papers. No one in Pointe-Bleue had a television set in the 1950s, and politicians didn't bother coming to see us.

Time passed at a slow and increasingly excruciating pace. The parade of men in dark suits with a preoccupied air continued. Most likely they all had important business to settle. More important than the loss of our young Innu on a far-off reserve. My strength began to desert me, yet I refused to give up.

At five o'clock on the dot, the secretary gathered up her belongings. I hadn't seen the man with the aquiline nose again. Clearly, I had been guilty of the sin of pride to think that I could convince someone like Duplessis to take an interest in the fate of my people.

I roamed through the city, walking aimlessly. Then I returned to the terrace next to Château Frontenac. Malek had once told me how the Innu would come to Quebec City to sell their pelts. Also, before the arrival of the French, they traded here with other nations, including the Mohawk. I tried to imagine the land back then. Not an easy thing to do. At the base of the cliff, stone and concrete had taken over. No trees or shores could be seen. Moored in the harbour, large ships spewed dark clouds into the sky. Dwellings advanced to the water's edge.

To the north, a papermill occupied the whole shore. In its yard, mountains of trees whose trunks had been stripped waited to be sent through the machines that would reduce them to pulp. Wood from our land met its end in this sorry way.

Below, suburbs stretched as far as the eye could see. How many people lived crowded together in those tightly packed houses, forming a compact, swarming mass? So this was progress with its smoking chimneys.

The mountains on the horizon reminded me that Nitassinan still existed for those who know to look for it. Following the river, one finds our villages, Essipit, Pessamit, Uashat Mak Mani-Utenam, Ekuantshiu Ministuk, Natashquan, Unamen-Shipu, Pakuashipi, Shehatshiu, Natuashish. Up other rivers, one reaches Matimekosh, Kawawachikamach and Pointe-Bleue — Mashteuiatsh in our language.

When night fell, I returned to my spot by the wall. Stretched out on the woollen blanket, I watched the stars above. They comforted me.

The next day, I woke feeling more tired than when I had lain down. It felt like this was taking forever.

The secretary ignored me. Most likely she took me for a madwoman. I probably was. But the memory of our dead children was stronger than my desire to return to my loved ones. The woman typed on and on. The click of her fingers on the keyboard filled the room, and I dozed off, rocked by that music. I don't know how long I slept, but the sound of hurried footsteps woke me. The man with the eagle nose walked by with two subservient-looking people trailing him. Once again, he shot a curious glance my way before sweeping into his office.

The conversation inside grew animated and raised voices could be heard through the thick door of varnished wood. Other men entered. After several hours, everyone had left but the boss. They spoke in low voices on their way out. No one smiled.

The hours ticked by, and I was readying myself to leave again when the secretary beckoned to me. I rushed over.

"The premier will see you."

She smiled. I felt a tightening in my chest.

FACE TO FACE

The farther the train sped from the city, the farther the houses grew apart, gradually leaving room for fields and, finally, the forest. The tracks threaded their way through the mountains while, as the kilometres went by, nature unfurled its austere beauty.

I was back where I belonged, amid the perfume of wood and fir boughs escorting me home to Thomas and my loved ones.

The meeting with the premier had lasted only a few minutes. Duplessis was busy writing when I entered his private domain and, without looking up, he gestured for me to take a seat on one of the chairs across from his desk. Light filtered through the window and flung itself against the wood-panelled walls. An atmosphere of tranquility reigned inside, in contrast to the picture I had formed of the man in my mind.

Once he had finished, the premier laid his piece of paper down in front of him. At last, he looked up. His face seemed gentler than in the pictures. His features, other than his nose, sharp as an eagle's beak, were harmonious, with arched eyebrows above eyes that shone with intelligence. His hair was combed to the side, and his carefully groomed moustache accentuated his delicate lips. A dimple in his chin gave him a fetching air.

Maurice Duplessis leaned back in his chair and slid his thumbs inside the vest he wore beneath his suit jacket. No one had ever looked at me so piercingly.

"What can I do for you, Madame?" he said in a gravelly voice.

I explained the purpose of my visit. I told him about the white men who would come onto the reserve, about their big cars and the children's deaths. He listened carefully. What I remember of the scene is a man in a dark three-piece suit and immaculately ironed shirt, a grey tie round his neck, sitting across from an Indian woman in long skirts, a beret pulled down low on her forehead. A strange tableau.

"As you know, Indians are wards of the federal government. I have no authority in the matter."

But I insisted. "The federal government isn't interested in us. And as far as I know, Pointe-Bleue is in Quebec. Six kilometres from Roberval, to be precise, which, as you know better than I do, is a Union Nationale riding."

Duplessis raised his eyebrows, a half-smile on his lips.

"How did you come all this way?"

"The railway passes next to where we live."

"That's a long haul."

I shrugged. "Not that long."

The premier asked me a few questions about Pointe-Bleue, but I didn't really know what to say.

How did you tell a man such as him, who worked in a building like the parliament and lived in a suite in the Château Frontenac, what life was like for the Innu of Pekuakami now? How did you tell him about the melancholy eating away at our hearts? For people like Maurice Duplessis, our world was a thing of the past. The future belonged to the corporations.

When we bade each other farewell, he shook my hand. His secretary wished me a safe trip home. Outside, by the sculpture representing a half-naked Indian family, I let the setting sun warm my skin a bit to give me strength.

The train forged full speed ahead, pulled by one of the new diesel locomotives. A modern train in the midst of an ancient forest.

In Pointe-Bleue, nothing had changed. Children played on the deserted streets. The wind stirred up the middle of the lake and waves threw themselves at the shore with a roar. Marie and Christine sat smoking by a campfire. They wrapped their arms round me and poured me a cup of Salada tea.

I told them about my trip. They were particularly interested in the crossing of what is now called Parc des Laurentides, an area they had often visited in their youth. I described the parliament, the premier's office, and his singular secretary. The houses made of stone and the tall walls of the citadel surrounding the city, the densely populated suburbs and the factories spewing their clouds of smoke into the sky. They had a hard time imagining so many people living together in the same place.

Anne-Marie, Virginie, and their children joined us, and I continued my tale. I told them about the sumptuous Château Frontenac terrace, about the great river, strong and tranquil, that flowed at its base toward Nitassinan. Virginie informed us that Thomas and the others expected they'd be back from the outfitters soon. The news was met with joy by all. Surrounded by my loved ones, I ate partridge soup and grilled hare, facing Pekuakami. Closing my eyes, I could imagine myself back in the Péribonka. As you grow old, memories become treasures.

A few weeks later, trucks carrying heavy loads of wood showed up in Pointe-Bleue. Workers climbed out and began unloading their cargo. Curious, people stepped out of their homes.

The men set to work. The song of sawing and hammering echoed. A few weeks later, they were done. The Pointe-Bleue reserve's dirt roads would continue to turn into rivers of mud when it rained. But now, on either side, wide sidewalks allowed pedestrians to go about their business while staying dry and, most of all, safe.

CIRCLE

In the 1950s, they finally closed down the Fort George Catholic residential school that our children had been sent to. After thirty years, the damage had already been done. Only the elders still spoke Innu-aimun. They spoke it among themselves, among the old folk, as the whites say.

The former pupils of the residential school were now adults. They had children of their own. But the residential school that had tried to kill the Indian in them had not taught them how to be parents. All it had left them with was grief in their hearts and fear in their bellies. Their children grew up around angry parents.

Several years after closing down the Fort George residential school on James Bay, they had the gall to open another one, in Pointe-Bleue. This time, they send young Attikamek here to be sure they, in turn, would be far from home, cut off from their families and their roots. The children arrive by train from Wemotaci, Manawan, or Opitciwan, distant communities. They step out with the same frightened look that we saw in our own children's eyes when the plane came for them.

We hear all kinds of stories about the goings-on there, of pupils—boys and girls—being abused by the priests, for instance. On our reserve before, many of the parents didn't believe their children when they told of the horrors visited on them by the white priests in Fort George. The Innu, who were so pious, could not imagine that priests would abuse defenceless children. Now the abuse is going on here, yet no one dares to do anything. Who would listen to us anyway?

In Pointe-Bleue today, children wear store-bought clothes and people live in homes with central heating and running water, except for me. The old barrel and its dented zinc cup hanging from a string are still all I need.

But once you have experienced anger, sorrow too perhaps, it never leaves you. You learn to live with it. Which may be what makes us Innu today. Unfortunately.

Seeking refuge by the lake, as I do this morning, soothes me, reminding me of who we were and who we still are. The easterly wind carries the perfumes of the Péribonka. As long as it all still exists in my heart, it lives on.

Pekuakami. Sometimes, I tell myself you are the one who has kept me alive, breathing into me the strength needed to face all the ordeals fate has placed in my path.

Pekuakami. Your smooth surface melds with the horizon this morning, the sun sees itself as though in a mirror and that mirror reflects all my memories back to me.

Grand-mère. The word my grandchildren and my great-grandchildren use for me. This is what I have become, when what I dreamt of becoming was a *kukum*. Sometimes, I worry for them. Today's world is crueler than the one you offered up to me, Thomas.

In the village, there is talk of teaching Innu-aimun in school, and I can see in my little ones' eyes the same pride that shone in Malek's, Daniel's, Marie's, Christine's. This gives me hope. Each of you has left me, one after the other, and my time too is reaching its end as over the years we become the sum of all those wounds that kill us softly…

Thomas, you left without warning one icy morning when the disease eating away at your lungs finally carried you off in one great gust of wind, leaving me alone beside your cold body. Twenty years already. I cannot believe I have lived all these years without kissing you. I have never been able to fill the void left by your absence.

Yet here and now, when I close my eyes and fill my lungs with the lake's heady fragrances, I feel your hand on my cheek. It slides down my neck, caresses my body tenderly, presses it up against yours. The salt of your skin, your taut muscles, your whole being quivering, aroused. Abandon. Intoxication. Loving me. So much. Until the very end.

Deserting me was your only betrayal, Thomas. But you were right, my love. Life is a circle. And it returns me to you. Always.

Almanda Siméon outside her house

Cobh (Queenstown), Ireland, 1875

The trunk held all that was left of their belongings, and John Carmichael buckled under its weight. The carter helped him lift and carry it. Her baby in her arms, Abbie sat beside her husband. She cast one last glance behind her. Wooden planks barred the windows of their shop. The young woman's heart ached.

"Hup!"

The whip snapped in the air, and obediently, the horse began to walk. The cart advanced slowly along rutted and near-deserted streets. Like many before them who had left to try their luck elsewhere, they passed by battered shutters and rundown facades.

For the longest time, Abigail and her husband refused to leave. They shared a love for fine fabric and hoped that John's business sense and his wife's magical fingers would allow them to weather the crisis. Encouraging signs had begun to appear, giving a glimpse of a more carefree future. The infestation that had devastated crops for a decade and caused unprecedented famine had ended at last. But a ravaged Ireland was still having trouble picking itself up again, and poverty continued to reign throughout.

With heavy hearts, the Carmichaels, like so many Irish before them, made the decision to close down their business and abandon everything to start over on the other side of the Atlantic. Abigail had hesitated because of her child, who was only three.

"Isn't she too young for this journey, John?"

"Look around us, Abbie," he said, his blue eyes locked on hers. "People are dying of starvation. We have to leave as soon as possible."

They sold their last bolts of fabric and the bit of furniture they owned to pay for the trip. Abbie had made warm clothing for the child as protection from the cold on a continent people characterized as a wilderness. She had spent the days leading up to their departure in a state of heightened excitement as she readied everything; now, sitting in the cart, the situation seemed unreal. She had hoped for a different destiny, but misfortune spared no one during these times of hardship in Ireland.

Feverish activity prevailed in the harbour. Steamships, their smokestacks spewing clouds of soot, sat side by side sailing ships. On bridges, crews busied themselves. The last passengers were boarding; some had no baggage other than the clothes on their backs. The old sailing vessel they were to travel on was docked at the end of the wharf, facing a row of cramped lodgings. They had to hurry. The carter helped John load their trunk onto the ship's bridge.

The grey-faced man waved goodbye. He had witnessed the departure of so many travellers.

The sailors cast off, and the wind swept into the sails, which began to flap. John held his child in his arms, his wife at his side. The city they had called home gradually receded. As far back as he could remember, his family had always been in commerce. It had allowed them to survive the famine. However, since 1845, hundreds of thousands of Irish nationals had left their country, forced to flee starvation, and many of those had travelled through Cobh. The harbour's activity had kept the economy going for a while, but business had collapsed.

Seeing so many people leave, John Carmichael had decided to try his luck too. The massive silhouette of Saint Colman's cathedral, being built on a hill from where it dominated the wharf, was the last image he would have of his homeland.

The ship sailed down the River Lee, then headed west, pushed by the wind. They'd been told that the crossing could take anywhere from five to nine weeks. Steamships could do it in less time, but this was the only vessel on which they had managed to secure a spot. Clutching the cross round her neck, Abbie pressed up close to her husband. Sick at heart, the pair watched the coast of Ireland gradually disappear on the horizon, knowing they would never see their homeland again.

The transatlantic companies that shipped wood from Canada to England often took on Irish emigrants for the return trip, crowding them together in insalubrious holds. John and his family were on an old three-masted barque that creaked in the waves. The Carmichaels settled on the between deck with the other travellers. John wondered if he'd been right to drag his wife and only daughter into this adventure. But what other choice had he had?

Life on the ship soon proved to be difficult. Crowded into the belly of the old craft, three hundred passengers suffocated in the semi-darkness. A pestilent stench invaded the deck, which had no sanitary facilities. The reek of the vessel permeated the travellers' flesh.

A week in, the westerly wind, which until then had been pushing them at a good clip, died. The ship drifted on a waveless sea. The heat and almost unbearable humidity sapped morale. The whole ship oozed.

The first to fall ill was an elderly man, already weak. A high fever felled him, forcing him to remain bedridden. Soon, red spots appeared and spread over his whole body. Everyone recognized the symptoms of the awful disease that had ravaged Europe. The traveller died shortly thereafter and his body was thrown into the sea. But typhus had erupted on board and panic spread through the ship. Whenever she could, Abbie took her child up onto the bridge. She hoped the sea air would purge her lungs and safeguard her. But the captain forced the passengers to stay below deck, where more and more people fell ill.

Abbie's throat seized up at the sight of the first spots on her husband's skin. John, who had not felt well for several days, hadn't wanted to worry his wife and had hidden his condition. Clutching her cross, Abigail prayed to Heaven to save him, but the spots spread over his whole body. One dark night, the fever bore him away. Abbie cried as she clung to the man with whom she had known so much happiness despite the hardships. At dawn, she stood by helplessly as the sailors threw his body into the ocean.

After four weeks of unbearable waiting, the wind returned and the ship was able to continue over stormy seas. Other typhus cases broke out, then the epidemic subsided as though the fresh air of the open sea had chased it away. After nine weeks, the coast appeared. A huge cry rang out on the bridge.

Soon the ship advanced between two rows of trees. To the south, Abbie caught a glimpse of towns and villages surrounded by fields. To the north, a coniferous forest formed an impenetrable barrier. What was this strange country they had reached, exhausted yet full of hope?

The ship dropped anchor at Grosse-Île. The immigrants were required to quarantine. After a shower and a proper cleaning-up, the passengers were led to their lodgings. Abbie and her child settled into a small, spotless bedroom. The light pouring through the window comforted her. She missed John. He would have loved this landscape of green hills surrounded by water that reminded her of their homeland.

At mealtimes, Abbie headed to the shore and lit a fire to cook the rations provided to her. Slowly, the young woman felt herself reborn next to this vast body of water and its fragrances of salt and grasses. In the afternoon, she walked through the forest as her child skipped among the trees.

Every day, Grosse-Île's lodgers had to submit to an intensive session of scrubbing and a medical exam. During one such inspection, the doctor discovered spots on the young woman's back. Hearing the diagnosis, Abbie felt as though she'd been punched in the stomach. The night swallowed her whole.

She was led with her child to another wing, the invalids' wing, lugubrious with its peeling walls and rudimentary furnishings. A raging fever took hold of her. Abbie started to slip away. Sometimes, in her delirium, John appeared, and she reached out to him. But her husband could not hear her cries, and fear slowly engulfed her. The last of her strength seeped away, it was hard for her to breathe. In one final effort, she sought out her daughter's face and her eyes, the same light, soothing blue as John's.

"What have I done? Why did I bring you here? What will become of you, my child, in this wild country? What will become of you, Almanda?"

A WORD FROM THE AUTHOR

Almanda and Thomas lie side by side in the Kateri Tekakwitha cemetery. There is a mistake on my great-grandmother's tombstone. Someone wrote "Amanda" there. The error most likely comes from the fact that everyone in Mashteuiatsh called her Manda. When I was younger, it bothered me. How could someone misspell the name of a woman who had lived to the age of ninety-seven? But now it makes me smile. Until the very end, the question of her origins will have sown seeds of doubt.

In fact, there are several versions of my *kukum's* ancestry. Some claim she was born in Nitassinan of an Innu mother. That her father, a French-Canadian, wed an Irishwoman for his second marriage, which would have led to confusion. Every story is equally valid. I have relied on the tale my mother has told me ever since I was a child.

Outside the village, the cemetery lies along Rue Mahikan on the side of a hill rising gently before Pekuakami. A small metal mesh fence separates it from the surrounding trees. It is ringed by a low stone wall, and an opening in the centre gives onto a dirt path. Cedars have been planted on either side of the entrance and a few other trees have been left standing.

It isn't one of those austerely beautiful cemeteries that people stroll through in surroundings conducive to reflection or that tourists visit to experience their dignified charm. The fence wobbles, the trees are poorly pruned, and dandelions dot the grass. Among the tombstones of grey and black granite with no order apparent in their placement, wooden crosses are planted in the sand in memory of the other women, men, and children who died and are buried on the land. Like my great-uncle Ernest.

The calm majesty that reigns in this sacred place suits the Innu spirit, and one feels at peace here in the heart of the boreal forest.

No one knows what happened to young Julienne Siméon after she was sent to Montréal. No one knows what illness it was she suffered from. One more secret. A few years ago, her sister Jeannette discovered that she had been buried in an unmarked grave in the Kahnawake cemetery. Jeannette brought stones from Île de Fort-George. She buried them there and erected a small mausoleum in memory of her sister.

My memories of Almanda Siméon are above all of a warm-hearted woman. She smiled a lot. Her eyes sparkled. She was curious and happy to see us, her great-grandchildren born in Alma, far from her.

During one visit to Pointe-Bleue, as it was still called at the time, someone took a picture. I see myself again, smiling behind my brothers and a cousin.

The author and his family in Mashteuiatsh

We, with my mother and my grandmother, are all gathered around Almanda. Four generations of the Siméon family stare into the same lens. Almanda holds herself tall. It's spring, she's wearing big rubber boots and the skirt with the coarse fabric on which she used to strike her match to light her pipe. We stand beside her little house across from the railroad tracks. Behind us, you can see the former presbytery, now gone.

That day, in a workshop adjoining the house, Gérard, Almanda's youngest son, was busy building a magnificent birchbark canoe, which left a huge impression on me.

In the picture, the blond hair of my youngest brother, Nicholas, and our cousin Luc stands out. A colour inherited from Almanda. My brother Éric and I have black hair like Thomas. Our oval faces and full lips are also Innu traits. But I like to think that it's from her that I inherited my love for books—and also perhaps the adventurous spirit that has served me so well in my profession as a journalist—as well as the deep attachment to roots planted in humus and sand.

Since this picture was taken, there has been a great deal of change in the community. The name Pointe-Bleue was abandoned in 1985 for Mashteuiatsh, meaning "Where the Headland Is." Gradually, the wounds left by colonization are healing, but its scars are still visible. Nothing, I'm afraid, will ever erase them entirely. One has to learn to live with them, and that road is a long one.

Almanda's little house still sits at the foot of the hill by the railway tracks across from the lake. I go back every time I pass through Mashteuiatsh. There have been renovations and additions. It has running water now. Family members still live there.

One day, my editor and friend Johanne Guay pointed out to me that everything I have ever written revolves around the issue of identity. I had never realized it. I asked myself why. Why this constant return to the past, to that heritage?

It is most likely because of the wound caused by the break with the past. By forcing women who married a white man to leave the reserve, the Indian Act tried to assimilate them. My brothers and I grew up in the city. We didn't learn Innu-aimun. They white-washed our ways, but who can forget the person he truly is?
Not I.

Montreal,
February 3, 2019

MICHEL JEAN is a writer, TV news anchor, and investigative journalist. The author of eleven books, he also writes and curates short stories and has edited two French-language collections showcasing Indigenous writers: *Amun* (2016) and *Wapke* (2021). In his 2012 novel *Elle et nous,* he opened up about his own Indigenous origins for the very first time. *Kukum* won the Prix France-Québec in 2020. Michel is Innu from Mashteuiatsh, and much of his writing reflects his Indigenous origins.

SUSAN OURIOU is an award-winning fiction writer and literary translator with over sixty translations and co-translations of fiction, non-fiction, children's, and young adult literature to her credit. She has won the Governor General's Literary Award for Translation, for which she has also been shortlisted on five other occasions. Many of her young adult translations have made the IBBY Honor List, including *Jane, the Fox and Me*, co-translated with Christelle Morelli. She has also published two novels, *Damselfish* and *Nathan*, and edited the anthologies *Beyond Words—Translating the World* and *Languages of Our Land—Indigenous Poems and Stories from Quebec*. Susan lives in Calgary, Alberta.